BLACKFOOT TERRITORY

Canyon looked warily about him. The wind high in the pines had dropped off. An uncanny silence had fallen over the forest. The muscles in his belly tightened.

The sound was so slight, he barely heard it—a moccasined foot crunching a tiny twig. He whirled to see the Blackfoot, a fleeting shadow among the pines, charging him, hatchet held high. Canyon flung up his Henry and got off a quick shot. It was too quick. The round ricocheted off a tree. Before Canyon could crank a new shell into the firing chamber, the Blackfoot struck him shoulder high, slamming him back against a tree trunk. And Canyon saw the savage's hatchet descending with murderous force.

When you fought a Blackfoot, you were either fast or dead . . .

CANYON O'GRADY RIDES ON

☐ **CANYON O'GRADY #8: BLEEDING KANSAS by Jon Sharpe.** The Kansas territory was due to be a state—if anyone survived the struggle to say if it would be slave or free. That's when the President sent in Canyon O'Grady to return the rule of law to this lawless land. (166108—$3.50)

☐ **CANYON O'GRADY #9: COUNTERFEIT MADAM by Jon Sharpe.** Canyon O'Grady rides into the town of Stillwater, hunting the source of a flood of phony government bonds that could drown the country in a sea of bad debt. (167252—$3.50)

☐ **CANYON O'GRADY #10: GREAT LAND SWINDLE by Jon Sharpe.** The redheaded law enforcer must stop a plot of assassination and landgrab. But first he must outshoot a swarm of savage shootists ... and outsmart a snake-slick politician. (168011—$3.50)

☐ **CANYON O'GRADY #11: SOLDIER'S SONG by Jon Sharpe.** Someone was giving Comanches government-issue guns ... somebody was giving the U.S. cavalry troopers a bloody taste of hell ... and somebody was going to pay when Canyon O'Grady found his target and pulled the trigger.... (168798—$3.50)

☐ **CANYON O'GRADY #12: RAILROAD RENEGADES by Jon Sharpe.** Canyon O'Grady knew that the President was targeted for death. Now Canyon must face the toughest challenge of his life ... to move faster than an assassin's bullet and unmask murderers who struck like lightning and burned with hellfire hate. (169212—$3.50)

☐ **CANYON O'GRADY #13: ASSASSIN'S TRAIL by Jon Sharpe.** Canyon has to catch up with the kingpin of an assassination ring making tracks for Oregon—and the trail cuts through dangerous Blackfood land! (169646—$3.50)

Buy them at your local bookstore or use this convenient coupon for ordering.

NEW AMERICAN LIBRARY
P.O. Box 999, Bergenfield, New Jersey 07621

Please send me the books I have checked above. I am enclosing $_____ (please add $1.00 to this order to cover postage and handling). Send check or money order—no cash or C.O.D.'s. Prices and numbers are subject to change without notice.

Name_____

Address_____

City _____ State _____ Zip Code _____

Allow 4-6 weeks for delivery.

This offer is subject to withdrawal without notice.

CANYON O'GRADY

13

ASSASSIN'S TRAIL

by

Jon Sharpe

Ⓢ

A SIGNET BOOK

SIGNET
Published by the Penguin Group
Penguin Books USA Inc., 375 Hudson Street,
New York, New York 10014, U.S.A.
Penguin Books Ltd, 27 Wrights Lane,
London W8 5TZ, England
Penguin Books Australia Ltd, Ringwood,
Victoria, Australia
Penguin Books Canada Ltd, 2801 John Street,
Markham, Ontario, Canada L3R 1B4
Penguin Books (N.Z.) Ltd, 182-190 Wairau Road,
Auckland 10, New Zealand

Penguin Books Ltd, Registered Offices:
Harmondsworth, Middlesex, England

First published by Signet, an imprint of New American Library,
a division of Penguin Books USA Inc.

First Printing, May, 1991
10 9 8 7 6 5 4 3 2 1

PUBLISHER'S NOTE
This is a work of fiction. Names, characters, places, and incidents either are
the product of the author's imagination or are used fictitiously, and any resemblance to actual persons, living or dead, events, or locales is entirely coinci-
dental.

Canyon O'Grady

His was a heritage of blackguards and poets, fighters and lovers, men who could draw a pistol and bed a lass with the same ease.

Freedom was a cry seared into Canyon O'Grady, justice a banner of his heart.

With the great wave of those who fled to America, the new land of hope and heartbreak, solace and savagery, he came to ride the untamed wildness of the Old West.

With a smile or a six-gun, Canyon O'Grady became a name feared by some and welcomed by others, but remembered by all . . .

1859, on the great trail stretching across savage and wild lands to the promise of prosperity and peace beside the Pacific . . .

1

As the tall, red-haired man strode through the ornate lobby of Cincinnati's most elegant hotel, he felt only a desire to be somewhere else. Marble walls enclosed a jungle of tall palms and bright-green rubber plants. Red damask wall hangings gave the cavernous lobby the aspect of an anteroom to hell. It was quite appropriate, what with all the perfumed women, the heavy coils of cigar smoke, and the general air of decadence and dissipation that hung over the place.

As he had been instructed, he did not pause at the front desk, but pushed through the crowded lobby and headed directly for the broad marble stairway and ascended to the second floor. At the end of a thickly carpeted hallway, he knocked on the door to room 212. At the sound of footsteps approaching the door, he stepped back. The footsteps halted.

"Who is it?" a heavy, cautious voice called.

"Canyon O'Grady."

The door was unlocked and pulled open. A U.S. Army officer stood by the door as Canyon entered. He stuck out his hand. Canyon shook it. The grip was firm, powerful.

"Captain Jeremy Bullock," the officer said, introducing himself.

Bullock closed the door and indicated with a brisk nod a dark-clad figure sitting in a black leather settee in front of the window, the ornate head of a walking stick enclosed in both hands, his stovepipe hat resting on the arm of the settee.

"Canyon, this gentleman is Mr. Denton Philbrick, assistant to the president. This man, Mr. Philbrick, is one of our best agents, Canyon O'Grady."

Philbrick bowed his head slightly in greeting and remained seated. Because of the settee's placement—directly in front of the bright window—he remained only a silhouette to Canyon.

"Please be seated, Mr. O'Grady," the man said in a deep, sonorous voice that was obviously accustomed to exercising authority. "The president has spoken of you, and I must admit his description was most apt. I'll let the good captain apprise you of the reason for this meeting."

"Very good, sir," said Captain Bullock.

O'Grady made himself comfortable in a velvet chair while the captain, pacing in front of him, began his story.

"Two weeks before, on a trip to Cincinnati to make a political address, the president—as the result of a timely tip—barely evaded an assassination attempt. Two of the conspirators were apprehended before the attempt, the third was cut down in the hotel room where he had secreted himself with a rifle. At the moment the secret-service men burst into his room, he was positioned at an open window, a rifle in his hands, the president exposed on the pavement below him."

"Close call."

"Yes."

"Then why do you need me?" Canyon asked.

"We stopped these three, yes. But the man who financed them is still at large, and remains a constant threat to the president. He must be apprehended before he can create any more mischief."

"He's that persistent, is he?"

The president's man spoke up then. "He maintains that he has been ruined as a result of the president's policies. He is a fanatic on the subject and will never be dissuaded from further attempts on the president's life—now or in the future. He has great financial resources. It would be a simple matter for him to finance any number of assassination teams. He cannot be ignored and must be dealt with."

"And who is this man?"

"Judge Fowler G. Langley," Philbrick said.

Canyon frowned. "That name sounds familiar to me."

"It should. The judge was once very high in the previous president's councils. He was the assistant secretary of state."

"Ah, yes. Before Mr. Buchanan's victory swept him and his cronies out of power. I assume you have leads on his whereabouts?"

Instead of replying to Canyon directly, Philbrick glanced at the captain.

The captain said, "One of our agents has ascertained that he has joined a wagon train heading for Oregon."

"He's on the run, then."

"Not necessarily. He is still a very wealthy man. In Oregon, we are told, he has powerful friends, and he will use them to insulate himself from the consequences of this botched assassination. Indeed, with his financial resources, he could easily become a senator from this new state. There is some talk of this already, we understand. As a political opponent of the president and his party, any attempt to discredit him after his appointment to the Senate will be seen as politically inspired and effectively squelched. The man will go scot-free.''

"You see," said Philbrick on the settee, "Langley can bide his time, build his national reputation, and when he feels the time is ripe, proceed with his next assassination attempt.''

"Langley is a ticking time bomb," the captain said. "And the next time he strikes, he might well succeed.''

"Do you have any proof that this man Langley was behind this plot to assassinate the president?''

"We have his personal threat.''

Canyon frowned. "That all?''

"It was made point-blank to the president himself. We also have the signed confessions of two of his co-conspirators. Unfortunately, they have since hung themselves in their jail cells. Of course, we got nothing at all from the third assassin, since, as we have already mentioned, he was killed by our agents.''

"And that's the long and the short of it?''

"Langley is guilty, Mr. O'Grady," Philbrick said, his soft, yet powerful voice filling the room. "There can be no doubt of that.''

"Will Langley be traveling alone?''

"He has a constant companion," Captain Bullock replied, "a small, mean little ferret of a man devoted to the judge. Langley has taken care of him since he was a boy. His name is Jake Gettis. He will stop at nothing to protect his master, and though he may not look it, he has a keen, ruthless intelligence."

"What exactly," said Canyon carefully, "is my assignment, gentlemen?"

"Your assignment is relatively simple," said the captain. "Overtake that wagon train, join it if possible, and keep Langley under surveillance. In Portland, you will be met by members of the secret service. They have already left for Oregon by way of the Isthmus of Panama and should be there when you arrive. At that time, you will help them apprehend the judge."

"But you will do so quietly," emphasized Philbrick. "Very quietly. We want no publicity. None at all."

"I am assuming you are planning to give Langley a fair trial."

"Yes, of course," broke in Philbrick. "Fair it will be. You may rest assured on that score, O'Grady. But it will be a quiet, military trial that will spare the president and this country the trauma of a scandal that could rip apart our entire political fabric."

"I'm sure you can see my position," Canyon reminded them. "And why I'm asking these questions."

"We can," boomed Philbrick, "and it proves you to be a cautious and a thoughtful man, which is all to the good. The question remains: will you take this assignment or must we get someone else?"

Canyon frowned, considering carefully his options. "All right," he said, "I'll take it."

"Good," Captain Bullock said, obviously relieved.

Philbrick leaned back, pleased as well. His voice rumbled at Canyon from the corner. "The president will be most gratified. He has the utmost confidence in you, O'Grady. As he told me, with you on the case, he is certain he has little more to fear from Langley."

The captain walked over to a desk, took a manila envelope off it, and handed it to Canyon. "You'll find in here all we know about Judge Langley," he said. "It also contains the information you'll need to make contact with our agents in Portland. I suggest you memorize the information, then destroy the material. We want no tracks leading back to us. I'm sure you understand."

O'Grady did not bother to look through the envelope's contents. He would have time enough to study the material later.

The captain cleared his throat. "There's just one more thing, Mr. O'Grady."

Canyon waited.

"This meeting never took place."

Canyon smiled sardonically. Nothing like politicians when it came to covering their asses.

The captain took a buckskin pouch off the top of the desk and handed it to Canyon. "There's enough gold here to ensure your safe journey westward," the captain said. "Use it wisely. This will have to do until you reach Oregon."

Canyon took the pouch and hefted it. It would be enough.

"How soon can you leave, Mr. O'Grady?" asked Philbrick.

Canyon stood up. "Putting this city behind me will be no problem at all. I'll be leaving first thing in the morning."

Fort Billings, at the foot of the Rockies, was the jumping-off outpost for settlers heading for Oregon, the new Promised Land. It was all a bustle with traders and blanket Indians and frontiersmen of all sizes and shapes, but as Canyon rode through the gates into the fort's inner courtyard, he saw no sign of any wagon trains getting ready to pull out. This was a disappointment. He was beginning to wonder if he was ever going to catch up to the wagon train that had left Independence a full month ago.

Leaving Cormac, his palomino, and the rest of his gear at the fort's livery, Canyon searched out the fort's factor, Frank MacDougal, whom he found in his office next to the trading post. Canyon presented a letter of introduction provided by Captain Bullock.

So tall was the man that he had gotten in the habit of moving about in the interior of the fort stooped over like an old man, and now even in his office, he tended to remain bent over. His ruddy face was long and dour. He had pale, gloomy eyes and was not smiling now as he returned the letter of introduction to Canyon and waved him into a chair by his desk, then folded his long frame into his swivel chair behind the desk.

"Them's impressive credentials, Mr. O'Grady," he said. "Of course you can count on all the cooperation it is in my power to extend. But you must admit that letter leaves a great deal of important information out." He smiled dourly. "Like who it is you're after."

"All I'll be needing from you, Mr. MacDougal," Canyon said, "is cooperation and some information. Nothing more, I assure you."

"What is it you want to know?"

"Did a wagon train leave here for Oregon recently?"

"Does it snow in the winter? Of course. Them fool wagon trains and their crazy people've been comin' in all summer."

"When did the last one roll out?"

"Two weeks ago."

"Was there a Judge Fowler G. Langley among the settlers?"

"He was one of them, all right." MacDougal leaned back in his chair, his shrewd eyes narrowing. Now he knew who Canyon was after. "Like many others, he was not happy with the new route the wagon master was so bound and determined to take."

"What did he think was wrong with it?" Canyon asked.

"A safer, more-traveled route would be through South Pass, but Deacon Brewster's route will take them close to Blackfoot country."

"Deacon Brewster is the wagon master?"

"Unfortunately, yes. A more headstrong, opinionated leader of his flock I have yet to meet. He's a bad man to mix up with the Blackfoot. Those Indians are a devilish crew who have managed to keep their land free of white trappers and settlers for the past three decades. A recent bout with smallpox has cut their numbers considerably, but they won't be down for long. They are as fierce and incorrigible a tribe of aborigines as God ever suffered to creep upon this earth.''

Canyon stood up. "Looks like I'll just have to catch up to that wagon train before the Blackfoot do.''

"Anything you need, Mr. O'Grady, just holler.''

"I'll be thanking you for that. Good day, sir.''

After leaving MacDougal, Canyon sought out the sutler's store and tavern for a much-needed drink. In the crowded, almost stifling interior, he was lucky to find one unoccupied table off in a corner, and he slumped down into his first chair in too many days.

The barkeep hurried over. "What'll it be, mister?''

"Something out of a bottle—not a barrel.''

"Sure thing,'' the barkeep said, wiping off the table swiftly with a filthy bar towel. "I got just the ticket, an unopened bottle of rum come straight from the Indies.''

"Let's have it, then.''

As the barkeep hurried off, Canyon saw the factor's bent body enter the place. He caught up to the barkeep as he approached the bar, said a few words to him, then ducked out again. At the same time Canyon noticed a small, gaunt-looking character sidling past him into the place. He was dressed in buckskins and a beaver-skin cap and carried a Hawken rifle. He carried himself like a man who knew this country. In fact, if Canyon wasn't mistaken, this might be one of the few remaining mountain men that still prowled the Rockies.

The little mountain man peered through the thick layers of smoke, looking for an empty table. Canyon caught his eye and waved to the man, indicating the empty chair at his table. The little man nodded agreeably and hurried over.

"Much obliged, mister," he said, sitting down. "This here watering hole is filled clear to the brim."

"It is that."

"My name's Sam Wilder," the little man said, reaching across the table to shake O'Grady's hand.

"Pleased to meet you, Sam. I'm Canyon O'Grady."

"Good to meet you, Canyon. What're you drinking?"

"The barkeep mentioned a bottle of rum."

"That'll do it for me, then."

The barkeep brought over the bottle and two mugs, having seen Sam Wilder join Canyon. As Canyon reached into his pocket for a coin to pay the man, the barkeep waved him off.

"MacDougal says your money's no good here, mister. Anything you want's on the house. And he said for me to tell you, he'll be joining you before long."

"Well, now," Sam said, looking with some astonishment at Canyon. "This is the first time that canny Scotsman ever gave anything away without a damn good reason."

Canyon unstoppered the bottle and filled the cups.

As Sam pulled his drink toward him, he asked, "You look fresh from the East, Canyon. But you don't look like no tenderfoot."

"I'll take that as a compliment."

"So it was meant."

Canyon understood how much Sam's curiosity was aroused by MacDougal's promise to join them, but he was too much of a gentleman to inquire openly. So they concentrated on drinking their fill and getting acquainted. Canyon outlined his desire to overtake the wagon train. Sam was just as apprehensive as MacDougal about Deacon Brewster's proposed route, but he pointed out that there was always a chance they would find help from the Nez Percé, traditional enemies of the Blackfoot.

Their discussion of the Blackfoot ended when they caught sight of MacDougal's tall, stooped figure making his way through the smoke and hubbub to their table. After a brisk, pleased nod to Canyon, MacDougal folded his long frame into a chair at their table, then turned his attention to Sam. "You got plans, Sam? I mean for the rest of this summer?"

"Sure, Mac. I'll be shootin' game for your winter larder. All I'll need is a little credit for supplies."

"Sam, if it's credit you want, you don't need to hunt game for it. Just come see me. I know you're good for it."

Sam leaned back in his chair and eyed MacDougal calculatingly. "That so, Mac? Sure is nice to hear. You givin' away any free cigars while you're at it?"

MacDougal did not reply. But his dour expression lightened some as he tamped fresh tobacco into his pipe and lit up. That accomplished, he turned his full attention on Canyon. "Seems I got me a real problem, O'Grady. Just after you left me, I had visitors. Official visitors."

"You can call me Canyon, MacDougal."

"And you can call me Mac. Anyway, it seems these three are what is known as a topographical-survey party from the U.S. government. They are searching for an easier, more direct passage over the divide. Seems like someone told them dunderheads in Washington that there was another pass north of South Pass. Looks to me like they'll be taking the same route as that wagon train that just left.''

''Hell,'' Sam said, ''there's no secret about them other passes. Everyone knows South Pass ain't the only one through them mountains, but pretty near all of them are decorated with white scalps—put there on purpose by the Blackfoot.''

''That's what I tried to tell them. But the captain of this survey party says he's got his orders.''

''He's a dumb, naked fool, then.''

''That's about the size of it,'' MacDougal agreed glumly, ''but he'd march through hell's front door if them were his orders.''

''Don't see what it has to do with me,'' Canyon said. ''If I were you, I'd give them whatever provisions they'll need, then wave good-bye. If they lose their topknots, that's their problem. You can't be expected to be a nursemaid to every crazy bunch of government topographers poking around out here.''

''Them's my sentiments exactly, Canyon. But there's a hitch this time.''

''What is it?''

''This party has a woman in it.''

''What the hell is she doing out here with a survey party?''

''She's a botanist. The way she tells it, she'll be keeping a journal for the government, illustrating all the strange and unusual flora she finds. But that ain't the only reason she's making this trip. She's on her way to kin living in Oregon.''

''Kin?''

''Her brother, a sea captain who's settled along the

coast. He's starting a town, and he's advertising for people from the East to settle in it.

"Canyon," said Mac after a pause, "I want you and Sam here to guide this survey party."

"I was wondering when you'd get around to that," Canyon said.

"Will you do it?"

"I got other business, Mac. Remember?"

"I know you got other business. And I sympathize. But hear me out. If you don't want to help these two topographers, help the girl. Besides, it seems to me you'll be going in the same direction as that wagon train you're after."

Canyon considered this, then looked intently at MacDougal. "That's tempting, Mac, but what makes you think this woman can make such a trip?"

"Because she won't take no for an answer, that's why. And she's come this far already."

"If she's got any sense, you can talk her out of it."

"Come dine with me tonight. You and Sam. In my quarters on the second floor. She'll be there. You can judge for yourself if she can be talked out of this fool trip."

"Fair enough."

"We dine at six."

"We'll be there."

"Fine. I'll be opening a fresh bottle that just arrived from St. Louis."

The bottle contained fine Kentucky bourbon and Canyon found himself and Sam sharing it with the two army surveyors and a tall young, green-eyed blonde in her early twenties. The two men were

Lieutenant Kurt Kingsley and his brother Second Lieutenant William Kingsley. Kurt was in charge since he outranked his brother. The woman's name was Kersten.

She was astonishingly beautiful, her cleanly sculpted features set off by high cheekbones, lips full and passionate, teeth like pearls. Rather than decorously parting her hair in the middle and wearing it in a bun behind her head, as was the style back East, she had combed out her long curls, allowing them to frolic down her back. Perhaps an inch or two taller than her escorts, she wore a green dress with a clutch of lace at her throat, the bodice fitting over a corset that reduced her waist's span considerably. Frilly petticoats peeked out from under her long emerald skirt.

After the introductions, Canyon slumped into an easy chair, content to study the three and keep his ears open. Lieutenant Kurt Kingsley was doing most of the talking. Canyon soon found he did not like the man much at all. He was a braggart—and worse. His younger brother William seemed concerned only with placating him, which was a shame; Kurt needed curbing badly.

Kurt was scathing in his portrait of the local aborigines, as he called them. He considered the lot of them the most miserable and benighted of all God's creatures. Even though Canyon could agree with some of Kurt's pronouncements, he found this man's arrogant assertiveness about a people he knew so little irritating in the extreme. He could tell that Sam Wilder felt the same way.

MacDougal tried to balance Kingsley's views somewhat, but the lieutenant wasn't having any. He swept all of Mac's comments aside with barely concealed scorn, while his brother, William, took every opportunity to second Kurt's remarks. The upshot of it all was that the only good Indian was a dead Indian.

Kersten, obviously amused by the two men's eager, foolish pronouncements, seemed content to stand back and observe, a tight, barely perceptible smile on her classic face.

When Canyon saw that poor MacDougal was about ready to blow his stack, he got out of his chair and, nudging Sam, walked over to the four.

Kurt turned at Canyon's approach and smiled condescendingly. "By all means, Mr. O'Grady. Do join the conversation."

"You don't seem to have much respect for the Indians," Canyon commented.

"Why should I?" Kurt demanded. "They are ignorant aborigines, benighted savages without culture. From what I hear, they will soon drink themselves into oblivion."

"So I've been hearing."

Sam Wilder stepped closer to them. "You sayin' they're *all* worthless?"

"Yes. And cowards to boot. There is entirely too much fear of them. It is generated, I am sure, by those who know nothing at all about their true nature. They are a filthy, degraded lot—and the sooner they are wiped out, the better it will be for all of us."

"All of them?" Canyon inquired.

"Yes, all of them." It was obvious Kurt was a man who, once having taken a position, could not easily be dislodged.

"No exceptions? None at all?"

"None."

"What about those white men who live with Indians, or who've been brought up by them?"

"Squaw men?" Kurt spat contemptuously. "They are no better. Indeed, perhaps they are worse, having turned on their own culture to ape the Indian in their manners and dress. But I understand their terrible dilemma. Once a white man becomes tainted with this savage culture, there is no turning back for him—for any of them. They too become savages. I would even suggest that such white men have lost their souls. They have submitted to the darkness of this wild land."

"You know this for a fact, do you?"

"Surely," said Kurt, "you two men must be aware of this. You can't be so foolish as to believe what so many romantic fools in the East believe. These aborigines are not noble savages."

"Well, now," drawled Sam, "you sure do paint with a broad brush, Lieutenant."

"How so, Mr. Wilder?"

"Well, now, take my wife, Mountain Lamb. She's a Shoshone, though some call 'em Snakes from the way their hand moves when they sign-talk. Anyway, all her people been friends to the whites since Lewis and Clark passed through here."

It was clear that the lieutenant was somewhat taken aback by Sam's unabashed admission that he was married to a Shoshone. But though he was now aware of his indiscretion in damning all squaw men, he was not so discomfited that he felt any need to apologize.

Mac spoke up then, in an effort to second Sam

and at the same time dampen somewhat the lieutenant's discomfiture. "Take the Crows," he said.
"They love to steal horses, but they are the hand-
somest Indians in the Rockies. And I've been trading
with them quite profitably for years."

"Exceptions that prove the rule," Kurt said.

"And what about you, Mr. O'Grady?" said Kersten, stepping toward them, a devilish gleam in her
eyes. "Do you also have an Indian woman for a
wife?"

"I haven't been out here that long, ma'am."

"Call me Kersten. And I'll call you Canyon."

"That'll suit me just fine."

MacDougal cleared his throat nervously. "Time
for me to admit why I have brought you all here this
evening."

"Yes, Mr. MacDougal, why have you?"

"These two men might possibly be convinced to
act as your guides through this wilderness and over
the divide as well."

"These two men?" Kurt demanded incredulously.
"What possible help could they be to us? We've gone
this far with little difficulty. I daresay we can manage
without any local help."

"Mr. Canyon is from the East," MacDougal said.

"All the more reason to ignore any advice he
might have concerning this land and the aborigines
who inhabit it," Kurt said.

"I must admit there's some truth in what you say,"
Canyon drawled. "Mac has asked Sam and me to
accompany your party. But if we do join you, it won't
be out of any consideration for you two."

"Then why would you?" Kurt demanded.

Canyon smiled coldly. "Because we are both convinced that if you two buffoons take Miss Kersten any farther into these mountains, she might not survive the experience.''

"Such insolence," said William.

"Amusing. Most amusing," said Kurt.

Kersten said nothing, noting Canyon's assertion with an amused smile. She obviously thought he might be overstating the case against the two shavetails escorting her. But not by very much.

MacDougal cleared his throat nervously. "Dinner awaits in the next room. Shall we go in?"

"Sure," Sam said quickly. "I could eat half a buffalo."

"And that's *just* what we'll be having," Mac told them, leading the way into the dining room. "Roasted hump ribs and boudins, with buffalo tongue to top it off."

"Boudins?" repeated young William Kingsley, frowning.

"That's right, sonny," Sam said to the second lieutenant. "Them's buffalo guts fried in bone marrow."

Canyon saw Kersten's face lose its color. Chuckling, he took her arm and escorted her into the dining room. As to whether or not he and Sam would be riding out with them the next morning, there was no need for any further discussion. MacDougal was right: Kersten was not going to let herself be convinced to remain at the fort. Come hell or high water, she was going on. Which meant Canyon and Sam would be going along, too.

The next morning, preparing to move out, Canyon got an unpleasant surprise. The left front foreleg of his palomino was swollen just above the fetlock. He called over the livery stable owner, who examined the swelling with great gentleness and care, then stood up to face Canyon.

"Looks worse'n it is," he pronounced. "It's an infection, though. I'll have to lance it, let it drain."

"That doesn't sound good."

"Wouldn't be, ordinarily. But these Crows got some poultice they make out of moss and mold they find under some pine trees."

"Mold?"

"Yeah, that's right. After I lance the leg, I'll just wrap the poultice around the fetlock, make sure the horse don't scrape it off, and sure as I'm standing here, that Injun medicine will drain out all that puss and heal that leg good as new."

"You sure of that?"

"I've seen it work more'n once. Heals wounds like magic."

"How long will it take?"

"Give me two weeks and he'll be as good as new."

"I haven't got that long."

"Well, I got a fine black I can let you have. And when you get back, this here palomino will be as good as new, as frisky as a yearlin', and rarin' to go."

"Where's the black?"

The owner led him to a clean, well-kept stall in the back and showed him the horse he had in mind. It was a fine, sleek piece of horseflesh, all right— but no match for his own Cormac. Still, it might do.

"How much?"

The owner pursed his lips and studied the black,

then reached over and patted its square, powerful chest. "Since you're goin' into Injun country, I figure maybe we should dicker awhile. There's a chance that you and this here black might just up and disappear on me."

"Which would leave you with a fine palomino."

The man wiped off his hands with a dirty cloth. "Let's go into the sutler's, where we can dicker in comfort."

"Suits me," said Canyon.

But as he and the stable owner left for the sutler's, Canyon was already resigned to paying a stiff price for the black and suffering through a long and painful separation from a powerful and durable mount that had stood him in good stead these many years.

2

A week later Canyon pulled his black to a halt and looked back. The rest of the packhorses were no longer in sight. Sam Wilder was scouting ahead, on the lookout for trouble; Kersten was keeping close beside him. An excellent horsewoman, she rode astride like a man and made no apologies for it. They were no longer in Shoshone country and not yet in Blackfoot country, but Sam had been pointing out to Canyon increasing Blackfoot signs, which meant it was horse-stealing time and the Blackfoot were on their way south to filch what ponies they could from the Bannocks and Nez Percé. And maybe count a few coup while they were at it.

For the past three days Canyon had kept off the ridges, staying in the gulleys and draws, following what dry streambeds they could find. It was tough going, since their way was blocked almost constantly by deadfalls and at times, by a junglelike tangle of undergrowth. It was unusually warm this early in the spring and perspiration poured off all of them in constant, soaking rivulets.

Nevertheless, Kersten kept up without complaint. It was Kurt and his younger brother, William, who were continually falling behind. Now they were back there somewhere, completely out of sight. With a silent curse, Canyon left the two packhorses he was leading, turned the black, and with Kersten keeping close alongside, rode back to see what in the hell was keeping the two army officers.

When he reached them, they were in a ravine Canyon had traversed earlier, one clogged with brush and deadfalls, a sheer rock wall at their back, a mountain stream tumbling past them. It was pleasantly cool and damp here on the ravine floor, far from the hot sun baking the clifftops above, so what the two brothers had done was dismount and take a break.

William was sitting on a flat table-sized boulder, gazing about him absently, while a few yards farther down, Kurt was inspecting the right front hoof of one of the packhorses. Canyon's guess was that Kurt had heard him coming and was occupying himself in this manner simply in order to give him an excuse for not keeping up with him and Kersten.

Canyon dismounted and, trailing his horse, picked his way carefully over the boulders and deadfalls to Kurt's side. William got up off the boulder and before Canyon reached them took a position beside his brother. Kersten reined in her horse, remained in the saddle, and hung back to watch.

"What's holding you two up?" Canyon asked Kurt.

"This horse had a stone in its shoe. I just removed it."

"That doesn't account for the distance you've fallen behind."

"The pace you're keeping is too much for these horses," Kurt complained.

"Too much for the horses or too much for you?"

"Look here, O'Grady, this is miserable country we're traveling through, especially down here in these gullies and ravines. I say we'd make a lot better time if we followed the ridges above us. And it would be a lot easier on the horses."

"You mean easy on yourself. You heard what Sam said. Once we show ourselves against the sky, we'll have visitors. So we're doing it Sam's way. We're keeping down here out of sight. Now mount up and get a move on. We've got to cover ten, maybe fifteen miles more today."

"I don't intend to ruin these packhorses, O'Grady," Kurt replied testily. "They've cost the U.S. government a pretty penny. We still have a long way yet to go. And let me remind you, O'Grady: I'm in charge of this survey party. This is a government operation. I don't take those sightings every morning and night for my health."

"You mean you're pulling rank?"

"Precisely."

"That's fine with me. I don't much enjoy escorting you two fools through this land. Neither does Sam. We'll pack our gear and take Kersten on ourselves. Suits me fine."

"You mean leave us here alone?" William bleated.

"No. You won't be alone, William. You'll have your brother here to lead the way. You'll both do fine, I'm sure."

"Hey, now, wait a minute," Kurt said, no longer so certain of his ground. "I didn't say you could just ride off and leave us."

"Well, now, if you'll be pulling rank on me, that's just what I'll be doing."

"But Kersten wouldn't go with you," William said. "She'd stay with us." He looked beyond Canyon to Kersten. "Isn't that true, Kersten?"

"Stay with you," Kersten retorted contemptuously. "You think I'm crazy? You two couldn't find your way out of a closet."

Kurt looked back at Canyon in some consternation. "All right, then, O'Grady. I'm not pulling rank on you. But, dammit, if we push these animals any harder, they'll only end up crow bait. Either way, we lose."

"Maybe so. But my way we only lose the horses."

"Guess he might be right at that, Kurt," suggested William.

"Keep out of this, Will," Kurt snarled.

"We've talked enough," Canyon told them. "Mount up and move out—or stay here on your own."

Canyon stepped into his saddle, wheeled his horse, and rode out of the ravine with Kersten. He said nothing to Kersten, but he was still fuming inwardly by the time they reached the packhorses.

With Blackfoot raiding parties as thick as grizzlies, according to Sam Wilder, this was no time to be dawdling. The Blackfoot were divided into three distinct groups. The bands farthest north, extending well into Canada, were the true Blackfoot. To the south of them were the Blood, with the Piegans making up the southernmost branch. Despite these separate divisions within the Blackfoot nation, the tribes united and fought as one against every neighboring tribe. At the moment, the only other tribe they tolerated were the Gros Ventres, and that, Sam Wilder was almost certain, could change at any time.

A fierce, warlike people, the Blackfoot lived for combat, delighting in the most audacious coups. One of their favorite tricks was to sneak into a village at night and, without raising an alarm, make off with an enemy tribesman's most-prized war pony, even if it were picketed in front of the brave's lodge. If it were a famous war chief's pony, all the better. Sam Wilder told of one Blackfoot warrior who had stolen into a Teton Sioux's tepee and taken the sleeping warrior's war hatchet from beside his couch, leaving a bloody Sioux scalp in payment.

Sam Wilder had had many dealings with the Blackfoot, none of them easy and all of them dangerous. He had been impressed by this proud, fierce people. Implacable to their enemies as they undoubtedly were, they were generous to a fault when it came to their own people. Blackfoot chiefs were known to give away prized war ponies to less fortunate braves, and Sam had assured Canyon that the worst thing a Blackfoot could say of another tribesman was that he thought more of what he owned than he did of his own people.

Accordingly, Canyon had no desire to tangle with the Blackfoot, not with these tenderfeet around his neck. But keeping out of trouble with those three in tow was not going to be easy. How the Kingsleys had managed to get Kersten this far without losing their heads, he would never be able to understand. It had to have been luck. Pure, blind luck.

But sooner or later, all luck changed.

Two days later, close to nightfall, Canyon glanced impatiently back along the draw they had been following for the last hour or so. The two brothers were

33

still not in sight, had not been for the past fifteen minutes or so. Kersten was riding beside him. He turned to her, fuming.

"Dammit, Kersten. Where the hell are those two?"

He saw a quickly repressed merriment in her eyes. "I thought you'd already seen them."

"Speak plain, woman."

She pointed up at a ridge to his right. Following her glance, Canyon saw the two men riding along at a brisk pace through a thin stand of pine. Even as he watched, they rode across a patch of sky, outlined clearly in the bright sunlight. Canyon groaned in frustration.

Sam Wilder appeared, riding hard, pointing up at the ridge as he came on.

"Dammit, Canyon," he cried. "Lookit them two damn fools up there!"

"I know. I just saw them, Sam."

"I thought you already told them blamed fools to stay off them ridges."

"Yes, he did," Kersten told Sam. "But that's a real stubborn pair up there."

"We'll make camp here, Sam," Canyon said wearily, "while I go bring them two down here."

"Just don't be easy on 'em, Canyon."

The agent spurred his horse up a steep game trail to the ridge and took after Kurt and his brother. When Kurt heard the clatter of Canyon's mount, he reined in and turned to watch him, a mocking smile on his face. William held up also.

Without a word, Canyon dismounted beside Kurt, reached up, and hauled him off his horse. As Kurt began to bluster, Canyon slapped him . . . hard. The blow was sufficient to stagger him. Outraged and humiliated by such treatment, he charged at Canyon, swinging wildly, furiously. Canyon blocked the man's furious barrage almost casually, then stepped in with a solid right cross to the man's jaw that rocked him clear to his boots. He followed it up with a crunching left into his right cheek. This blow was enough to send Kurt stumbling backward to the ground.

"Here, you," cried William, rushing at Canyon. "Leave Kurt alone!"

Canyon brushed the younger brother roughly aside, then reaching down, grabbed Kurt's shirt front and hauled him back up onto his feet.

Woozy, Kurt stood before Canyon holding his jaw, considerably chastened by his swift, neat lesson in obedience. "You had no call to do that, O'Grady," he muttered bitterly.

"Didn't I?"

"I just sort of . . . drifted up onto this ridge. It was easy going, a damn sight easier than through that gully."

"That's not the point."

"All right. All right. Keep your hands off me, and I'll stay behind you from here on in."

"Do I have your word on that?"

"You have my word, dammit."

"Good."

"But there's just one thing, O'Grady."

"What's that?"

"I'll settle up with you later."

"Fine. Now get your ass back on that horse and move off this ridge."

Sullenly, but saying nothing, Kurt mounted up,

grabbed the packhorses' leads, and with his brother close behind, followed Canyon off the ridge.

Late the next day, Canyon found Sam Wilder waiting for him beside the trail.

"Hold up, hoss," he said.

Canyon pulled up beside him. "What's the problem, Sam?"

"We got a guest."

"A guest, is it?"

"Yep. A lone Blackfoot. He's been tailin' us for the past hour. He's waiting for a good chance to drop off and bring his fellows."

"I'll take care of him," Canyon said. "You keep an eye on these three innocent children until I get back."

Sam's eyes twinkled. "I think maybe you got the easiest job."

Canyon tossed the packhorses' reins to Sam.

"Which way is he, Sam?"

"Behind me on the ridge. He's ridin' a paint."

Canyon spurred his black past Sam and pushed it up the steep slope, keeping alert for any sign of the Blackfoot. When he did catch sight of movement in the pines atop the ridge, he dismounted swiftly, snaked his rifle from his sling, and moved on up the slope until he was deep in the timber just below the ridge.

Abruptly, the forested slope went silent. That meant danger. But as yet he had seen no further movement in the pines. Perhaps that had only been his overworked imagination. He held up and looked warily about him. The wind high in the pines seemed to have dropped off, an uncanny silence falling over the ridge. He felt his nerve endings tingling, the muscles in his belly tightening.

He was within sight of the ridge by now and started up again, moving in a crouch, darting from tree to tree, visible only as a shifting patch of buckskin. Again he held up, aware of the hair on the back of his neck lifting.

Something was coming at him. He was almost certain of it. But from what direction?

The sound was so slight, he barely heard it—that of a moccasined foot crunching down on a tiny twig. He whirled to see the Blackfoot, a fleeting shadow among the pines, charging him, hatchet held high. Canyon flung up his rifle and got off a quick shot. It was too quick, too hasty a shot. The round ricocheted off a tree. The Blackfoot kept coming, and before Canyon could crank a new shell into the firing chamber, the Blackfoot struck him shoulder-high, driving him back, slamming him back against a tree trunk. Canyon saw the hatchet descending with murderous force. At the last minute the agent ducked aside. The blade bit deeply into the tree. As the Indian tried to yank it free, Canyon fell back and, wielding the rifle like a club, whacked the man in the ribs with such force that he dropped to his knees and buckled over. Swiftly, Canyon cranked a fresh charge into his rifle and shoved the barrel into the Blackfoot's face.

On his knees the man looked up into the rifle's bore and waited for Canyon to pull the trigger—doing so without a whine for mercy, with a quiet, incredible courage that Canyon could only find it in his heart to admire.

Slowly, against his better judgment, Canyon

stepped back and lowered the rifle. "Get up," he told the Blackfoot.

The Indian frowned angrily. "You will not kill me?"

Surprised at the Indian's command of English, Canyon said, "No. I give you back your life. You are a brave man. Let me and my four companions move through your country in peace. We mean no harm."

The Indian stood up quickly and smiled, his white teeth bright in his dark face. But there was neither gratitude nor pleasure in his smile. He seemed to exude hostility, not gratitude.

"You are a fool, white man. Eagle Feather does not want the gift of life from such as you."

"Hell, man," Canyon reasoned. "You don't even know me."

"I know and hate all white men. They took me when I was a boy and taught me in their schools. But all they teach are lies. They defile the land of my ancestors. They have no honor. When they die, their souls beg for mercy. They are nothing but a pestilence on my land and my people. I am sorry I did not kill you. The next time we meet, I will not be so unlucky."

Eagle Feather turned abruptly and raced back through the pines. For a few seconds longer, he was visible. Then he vanished among the other shadows of the pine forest.

Unsettled by the man's intense hatred, Canyon proceeded back down the slope to his horse. He had found an enemy, he realized, one who would never rest until he had redeemed the dishonor of having his life given back to him by a white man. It was a curious thing indeed. Had he not shown mercy, had he pulled the rifle's trigger, Canyon would now be a much safer man—as would all those in his company.

He had been a fool.

But not the next time—and he knew for sure that there would be a next time . . .

Later that night Canyon bedded down on a ridge above the campsite. The two brothers and Kersten were sleeping on the slope below, with Sam Wilder on the ridge opposite—sleeping as lightly as himself, Canyon had no doubt. After Canyon told him of his encounter with Eagle Feather, Sam had spat out a glob of tobacco juice and shaken his head. That had been his only reaction. He didn't have to tell Canyon he had been a fool, that was already understood. But he did say that now they would all have to keep a sharp lookout, even though Sam figured them to be still inside Nez Percé lands.

A revolver under his saddle, which he was using for a pillow, his rifle by his side, Canyon was almost asleep when he heard movement in the brush to his right. Slowly, stealthily, he tightened his hands on the butt of his revolver. A twig snapped. He flung himself around and swung up his handgun.

"Don't shoot," Kersten whispered hoarsely.

She was standing at his feet in the moonlight, her long golden hair cascading down over her pale night-gown.

"Tarnation, woman," Canyon said, lowering his gun. "I almost blew your head off. You mind explaining what in the hell you're doing up here?"

She lowered herself to her knees beside him. "You mean you don't know?"

"That Blackfoot I met this afternoon has made me nervous. And maybe you should be, too."

"I am. Believe me. But I'm also a woman."

"I'm not going to deny that."

"You see, Canyon, it's like this—Kurt wants to marry me."

"Kurt?"

"Yes. I think we're engaged. At least he says we are."

"You sure that's what you want?"

"I must admit, at first he . . . intrigued me."

"I see."

"But not any longer, I assure you."

"Why's that?"

"My God, haven't you noticed? Kurt is a fatuous idiot."

Canyon smiled. "Just discovered that, have you?"

"Not just. The certainty of it has been coming on steadily, ever since we left the fort."

"In this country, Kersten, he could be very dangerous."

"Don't you think I know that?"

"So what do you want from me?"

"Comfort." She moved closer.

He could smell the body heat coming from her, and in the moon's dim light, the voluptuous swell of her breasts pushing against her nightdress caused his mouth to go suddenly dry. All he would have to do, he realized, was reach out and take one of those warm globes in his hand and feel its hard nipple digging into his palm, then pull her to him.

And so he did.

Cupping one of her breasts gently in his big hand, he pulled her to him. She came forward with a sigh, opened her nightgown for him, and pressed herself against him. He was as naked as she in less than a moment, and the feel of her skin against his was almost overpowering. He swung her onto his bedroll and mounted her slowly, taking in her incandescent loveliness as he did so, his eyes drinking it all in. Her lips were parting and waiting for him to drink deep. He closed his lips over hers and, leaning close upon her, felt one breast against his chest, the nipple firm, thrusting. Inside his mouth her tongue came alive, darting, circling, teasing, awakening a sharp, excited response in his groin.

He pulled his lips away from hers and dropped them upon one of her breasts, circling the hardening tip with his tongue, the flesh about the areola, drawing her full breast deeper into his mouth, pulling on it teasingly, until she cried out softly.

"Now, my love, now. Enter me. Do it now!"

She thrust her curly nap eagerly up at him and he found himself more than ready. With a quick, delighted lunge he buried himself deep into her smooth, lubricious pathway, and her answering moan of pleasure seemed to fill the night. He thrust forward deeply, fully into the scalding tunnel that tightened convulsively about his erection, as firm as a fist. She grabbed his shoulders and moaned with delight, her body rocking lasciviously under him, her arms reaching out to encircle his neck and bring his face down into the hot valley between her breasts. And then she was tossing her head from side to side, her eyes wild, her face taut, meeting him thrust for thrust, the two of them flying at each other like wild things.

"Now, Canyon, now," she whispered savagely. "I'm coming! Don't stop now. Please!"

She had no need to instruct him; on the road they had taken there was no turning back. He became a wild man himself, thrusting at her with a brutal, insistent fury as he plunged toward his own climax, barely aware now of the blond creature tossing and crying out beneath him . . . and like a racehorse sweeping past the pack, he burst across the line, climaxing in a series of wild, gushing pulsations that left him weak.

And thoroughly satiated.

He looked down, to see Kersten smiling happily up at him.

"Is this not a delightful thing we do, you crazy Irishman?"

"It is that, lass."

"For a while, I thought I lost you."

"I did get carried away then, didn't I? And for that I thank you."

"Kersten!"

It was Kurt, on the slope below them. He had evidently awakened and, seeing she was not in her sleeping bag, had got up to investigate. He sounded worried. In a moment his brother could be heard stirring as well.

"Those fools," Kersten said. "They'll wake the dead."

She kissed Canyon full on the lips, then slipped back into her nightgown and hurried off down the slope.

Two mornings later, Canyon was standing beside Kurt watching the man fold the tripod that a moment before had held his theodolite. The lieutenant had just finished recording the morning transit in his notebook. Sam Wilder had meanwhile ridden off to scout the trail ahead. Farther down the slope Kersten was bent over her pad, her brush moving swiftly, deftly as she painted some wildflowers she had discovered earlier. Canyon had looked over many of her renderings by now and was quite impressed by her skill as an artist as well as her knowledge of botany.

The morning was beautiful, with small rafts of cumulus clouds drifting across a radiant blue sky. Venus still gleamed in the heavens. The call of birds and the chatter of squirrels and chipmunks echoed in the treetops overhead as they leapt from branch to branch, while high above them in the tops of the pines, the wind sounded like surf on a distant shore.

Kurt hefted the folded tripod onto his shoulder. "I'm finished," he said, and started down the trail.

Canyon remained back to check the encircling horizon once more. It remained clear. No smoke lifted from any camp fire that he could see. Satisfied, he followed after Kurt. He was halfway down the slope when he saw a thin tracery of smoke rising from their own campsite. Though it soon dissipated once it cleared the ridge, Canyon knew it would still be visible for miles.

Cutting past Kurt, he ran down the trail and into the campsite, where William was kneeling beside the fire, pouring himself a cup of coffee. Canyon kicked the coffeepot out of his hand, then kicked away the blazing firewood and stomped out what embers remained. Then he whirled on William, who was now casting nervous glances up the slope at his brother.

Kurt was still lugging the tripod, but he was hurrying toward them as fast as he could. Kersten, her notebook and paint box tucked under one arm, was picking her way swiftly down toward them as well.

"Damn you, William," Canyon said. "Sam said there was to be no camp fire this morning."

"But Kersten said she wanted some hot coffee for a change."

"I don't give a damn what Kersten wanted."

"He's right," Kersten said, pulling up beside Canyon. "It's my fault. I'm sick of these cold camps. I asked him to heat up some coffee."

Canyon turned to her. "I don't blame you for asking. I blame him for lighting the fire."

"I'll handle this," said Kurt, putting down the tripod and the rest of his gear. "I'm still in charge here."

"Then take charge," Canyon told him. "This fool brother of yours has just invited any Blackfoot war party in the vicinity to come join us. That smoke could have been seen for ten, maybe twenty miles."

"I'm sorry," William told Canyon. The young man was obviously crestfallen. "I just thought I could make the fire without all that smoke. I've seen it done."

"You're right," Canyon told him, his tone less abrasive. "It is possible. But you have to burn dry aspen, not that punk pine kindling you were using."

"Yeah, Will," Kurt said with a grin. "Next time use aspen."

Wearily, Canyon turned away from the two. It was useless dealing with these two. Perhaps if they had confronted Eagle Feather as he had, they would understand what they were dealing with as they kept on into this wild land. But they did not understand and were bound and determined to press their luck. The trouble was that it wasn't only their luck they were pressing; it was his, Kersten's, and Sam Wilder's as well.

The following day, a little before noon, the narrow canyon they were following opened up onto a clearing and they found themselves riding alongside a broad mountain stream. This was indeed a shining land, Canyon told himself as he gazed down into water so clean it was almost invisible. Trout and smaller fish whisked and scooted about in its pristine depths, its pebbled streambed as clear as crystal.

"Keep a lookout for grizzlies," Canyon called back to Kurt and William. "Sam says the woods are full of them now, and they'll be coming down to this stream for the fish."

Riding alongside Canyon, Kersten laughed softly. "You think they'll believe you? I'm sure Kurt has not seen a bear he couldn't handle."

Canyon chuckled, even though he didn't find Kurt's manner all that amusing. The man seemed to have absolutely no conception of the world through which he was traveling. The only thing he saw and truly understood, it seemed, were those measurements he made every morning and evening through his theodolite.

The stream broadened abruptly and Canyon reined to a halt. Sam Wilder had ridden ahead about an hour back, and Canyon decided this would be a fine spot to make camp and wait for Sam to get back to them. There had been so much sign of Blackfoot—on every hand, almost—that Canyon did not like being separated from Sam for too long a time. Canyon and Kersten dismounted. Kersten slapped the rump of her mount, sending it toward the stream to slake its throat. In that instant, just as Kurt and William slipped wearily off their mounts as well, Sam Wilder burst out of the pines on the other side of the stream.

"Blackfoot," he cried, driving his horse across the stream. "Get out of here!"

As Sam gained the bank and whipped past them, Canyon leapt back onto his horse, reached down, and swung Kersten up behind him. Wheeling the black, he charged back the way they had come, hoping to regain the canyon before the Blackfoot cut them off. Behind him came a wild chorus of Blackfoot war cries, and glancing back, he saw mounted Blackfoot warriors charging across the stream after them. Kurt and his brother were hastily mounting up to follow after Canyon, but they weren't moving nearly as fast as they should.

Ahead of Canyon, Sam Wilder was charging full-tilt into the canyon and in a moment had disappeared entirely. As Canyon took after him, two Blackfoot broke from the pines flanking the trail and, whooping wildly, charged directly at Canyon.

"Hang on," Canyon told Kersten. "We can't go around these two; we'll have to go through them."

The closest Blackfoot nocked his arrow and drew back his bowstring. Canyon had already drawn his revolver and fired point-blank at the Blackfoot. The top of his head vanished and he toppled back off his pony. His second shot took out the other warrior, catching him full in the chest and slamming him sideways. Twisting his pony under him, he went down, and Canyon had a clear shot at the canyon's entrance.

Galloping into it, he saw no sign of Sam Wilder. He cut for cover close under the canyon's nearest wall, for with Kersten's added weight, there was no way Canyon's mount could outdistance the Blackfoot pouring after them. His only course was to gain what high ground he could and set himself up behind solid cover. Sighting a game trail, he followed it through a patch of scrub pine and up the steep, talus-littered slope beyond.

The black performed magnificently and would have been able to carry Canyon clear to the canyon's rim if it had not had to contend with a second rider. Less than two hundred yards from the rim, the black gave out and, uttering a strangled scream of despair, shuddered and flung itself sideways. The Henry rifle clutched in his left hand, Canyon grabbed Kersten with the other and leapt clear of the tumbling horse.

Dragging Kersten brutally up the slope after him, Canyon scrambled toward the rim, ignoring her cries that she could not keep up. At times he was forced to drag her bodily after him over sharp rocks and through gravel-lined gullies. Only when he at last scrambled up onto the canyon's rim did he let her go. Sobbing with exhaustion, she sank to the ground. He ducked back to the edge of the rim and peered down.

Showing more enthusiasm than good sense, the howling Blackfoot, most of them still on their ponies, were toiling up the steep trail after them. Calmly Canyon centered the Henry's sights on the closest brave's chest and pulled the trigger, planting a neat hole in his chest, the force of the charge car-

47

rying the Indian violently backward down the steep slope.

Another Blackfoot surged up the slope. He was a fine horseman, and it appeared he was going to be able to boot his pony all the way to the rim—until Canyon cranked, aimed, and fired in one swift motion, catching the pony in the chest, stopping it in midstride. Before the Indian could jump clear, the dead horse took him with it as it tumbled wildly back down the steep slope, cutting a wide, devastating swath through the ranks of the warriors riding up the slope behind him.

Canyon figured he had time now to make his move, and hurried back to Kersten. Still weeping, she had remained sprawled on the ground, her knees and elbows bloody.

"Look at me," she cried.

"That's nothing to what a Blackfoot will do when he gets hold of you. Get up!"

"I can't! I can't move."

"Then stay here."

She was shocked. "You mean you'd leave me?"

"Why not? You'll maybe give these bastards enough diversion to let me get clean away." As he spoke, he looked coldly down at her. This was no game. No eastern writer's pretty romance. This was either life or a horrible, prolonged death. And there was no time for discussion. His brutal words were calculated to shock her into realizing this.

He turned and ran in a steady, ground-devouring stride toward the cover of scrub pine a hundred or so yards back from the canyon's rim. He was almost to them when he heard Kersten's lighter footsteps behind him, her curses coming in breathless spurts as she labored to catch up to him. Once she did, he grinned at her and flung her down behind a bush, then glanced back, waiting for the first Blackfoot to gain the canyon's rim.

The one who did was a big fellow with a face streaked with black and white war paint. Canyon blew his head off his shoulders, cranked a fresh cartridge into the Henry, then pulled Kersten to her feet and dashed on through the scrub pine. This time she did not complain as she struggled to keep up with him.

At the far side of the scrub pine, a gentle wooded slope opened up before them, leading down to a thickly forested valley. What Canyon noticed at once was the abundance of cover it offered. Lodgepole pine and bushes, along with willow and aspen, crowded its slopes. There would be grizzlies in there as well, but that did not concern Canyon now. He would seek shelter in the devil's lair itself if that was what it took to shake off this pack of howling devils on their tail.

Pulling Kersten after him, he plunged down the slope and into the trees.

3

This band of Blackfoot, the Gray Lodges, had come from the eastern plains a year earlier during the Time of the Trembling Leaves. Harried by the Sioux, who had treacherously allied themselves with the Mandan and the Hidatsa, their best war chiefs and most courageous warriors decimated by the blanket sickness, the Gray Lodges had fled into the timbered foothills of the Rockies. Here they had set down their lodgepoles and secured for themselves new hunting grounds, daring the Nez Percé, the Bannock, or the Shoshone to dislodge them.

During the winter, deep in these wooded valleys and surrounded by the awesome, unapproachable snow-capped peaks, the people of the Gray Lodges felt cramped and out of touch with the spirits of their ancestors they had left on the plains. Still, as their camp chief Lame Buffalo pointed out, the spotted death that had struck down so many of their people had not touched those of their enemies who dwelt in this high, wooded land. Here they would find refuge as well; they would take this land for their children and hold it against all who would try to dislodge them. Besides, as the few remaining chiefs reminded one another in council, now they would not have so far to ride if they wished to count coup on their enemies or steal the handsome Appaloosa of the filthy Nez Percé.

Two sleeps before the attack on Big Shoulders and his small party, Eagle Feather entered Lame Buffalo's lodge with great respect, sat down, and accepted the pipe offered him. The two smoked awhile, exchanging the usual compliments before getting down to business. It was Eagle Feather who spoke first, remarking on the scarcity of lodges and the fact that so few warriors—and even fewer children—seemed to be about as a result of the band's recent misfortunes.

Lame Buffalo nodded solemnly, his eyes reflecting the sorrow he felt as he contemplated the terrible affliction that had wiped out so many of his people.

"It is our own fault that we deal with these white men," Eagle Feather told the chief. "It is they who bring such death upon us. We must keep away from their trading places. Evil things await the Blackfoot there. Stupid Water and all manner of pestilence such as that which goes from woman to man and man to woman."

"What you say is true, Eagle Feather. But the Blackfoot must have the white trader's goods, his knives, his blankets, his rifles, his steel, his arrowheads and awls, his shining glass."

"Why do you not take it from the white men who travel through our land?"

Lame Buffalo shook his head sadly. "There are not enough white men to steal from in this country."

Eagle Feather said, "You know of me, Lame Buffalo. I am a lost child of the Blackfoot, stolen as a boy by the white-eyes. I do not know if any of my mother's band still survives. Only since this winter have I come here to join your people, and I am grateful to your hospitality."

"It is nothing," protested Lame Buffalo.

"I have lived in the white-eyes' lodges, gone to their schools, traveled far on their steamboats. Their towns, as they call them, are filled with muddy streets foul with horse dung and steaming piss. They live in wooden lodges with stone chimneys to let the smoke escape. They have windows of glass to look out of. And the stench of the white men is everywhere." Eagle Feather leaned forward as he spoke, eyes filled with hate. "We must not let these white-eyes into our country."

"We kill them and still they come," reminded the old chief. "No one can defeat them. They are as numerous as the sand that blows in the wind, that shift and move on but never diminish."

"Lame Buffalo is wise. And what he says is true. But we must not go quietly. We must fight back or we will lose our spirit. Even now, the white-eyes are moving closer to the people of the Gray Lodges. I have seen them. They are the bluecoats, the white man's warriors, and they measure this land to make it ready for settlement. I have seen this with my own eyes."

Lame Buffalo frowned, his anthracite eyes troubled. "If this is so, much evil will come to my people. But why do you speak to Lame Buffalo of this matter now?"

"I would lead a war party to capture these white-eyes. We will take their three-legged machine that measures the distance between peaks and valleys and destroy it. Then we will end the lives of those who would give our land to the filthy settlers.''

"Why do you feel you should lead such a war party? You have been with our band only a little while.''

"I have listened to the voice of my *puha,*" Eagle Feather replied solemnly.

The old chief nodded. "One must always listen to the voice of one's *puha.*"

"My helper has not failed me yet.''

Lame Buffalo considered Eagle Feather's words. It was true, he realized, that they must discourage settlement of their lands, but any encounter with hostile whites now would most likely deplete still further the ranks of his few remaining warriors and war chiefs.

Lame Buffalo spoke carefully. "I am only the camp chief. Tonight you will speak to the members of the chiefs' council. We will let them decide.''

"Will I have the support of Lame Buffalo?''

"You will have from this old chief whatever the council decides,'' Lame Buffalo told him craftily. Then he reached for his pipe, signifying that the discussion had ended.

Eagle Feather thanked the old chief for the audience and left promptly.

That night, with Eagle Feather's pent-up fury for the white men giving him an eloquence that turned all argument aside, the council of war chiefs decided that one way to change their own *puha* was to attack this small party of intruders moving through their land.

But the chiefs decided that not Eagle Feather, but

53

a war chief of their own choosing would lead the war party.

The next day Blackfoot scouts investigating a thin column of smoke rising from a single camp fire discovered that it was just as Eagle Feather had warned: a small party was heading through the mountains toward them. Returning in great excitement, the scouts spread the word and that night the skin drums were brought out and the warriors danced the war dance with a maniacal urgency they had never shown before, sending up cries that must have reached clear to the moon, their women urging them on, on occasion even joining them in the dance. The oldest war chief called up the ancient spirits of their band, and the young warriors shouted out bold promises to their women. Surely now whatever taboo the band had broken to cause their decimation by the blanket pestilence would be forgiven and their medicine would return, more powerful than ever.

The next day Eagle Feather watched from a nearby ridge as the Gray Lodges' most prestigious war chief, White Fox, led the attack on the small band. Moving through the tall grass like the lobo wolf of his spirit quest, he saw at once why this Blackfoot band enjoyed such poor luck. Instead of attacking while Big Shoulders and his party were still in the canyon, White Fox waited until after they had left the canyon so that not until the party reached the stream did they attack—and only then after it had allowed the mountain man to warn them.

The result was predictable. Big Shoulders and the white woman, and the mountain man as well, managed to escape back into the canyon.

Seeing how badly things were going, Eagle Feather sprang onto his pony to join in the pursuit of Big Shoulders. Reaching the canyon, he rode up the steep slope after Big Shoulders, but close to the rim he was knocked from his mount by a dead pony tumbling back down the slope, a thrashing avalanche of sinew and bone that almost knocked him senseless.

By the time he made it to the canyon rim, the Blackfoot warriors had lost four more of their number, and Big Shoulders, fleeing on foot with the white woman, had vanished. Eagle Feather ran through a stand of scrub pine and managed to catch a glimpse of Big Shoulders vanishing into a patch of alders on the flanks of the valley far below him.

At that moment two Gray Lodge warriors pounded up beside him, their chests heaving as they gulped in air.

"Big Shoulders has escaped," Eagle Feather cried, pointing to the line of trees into which he and the woman had just disappeared.

The two warriors could tell from the scorn in Eagle Feather's tone the contempt he had for their bungling of this ambush. But his anger was easily matched by their own. Many brave warriors, including the famed war chief White Fox, had been lost this day. Hatred flared in their eyes for this strange Blackfoot orphan who had joined their band to bring such a disaster upon them.

They turned on their heels and left him.

For them, at least, the pursuit of Big Shoulders had ended.

Howling like demons in torment, the bereaved women dragged the dead bodies of their warrior husbands from the backs of their ponies. Howling like animals and mutilating themselves with fine ingenuity, the bereaved squaws seemed to have gone mad with grief. One took up her head warrior's war hatchet and with a single stroke took off all the fingers on her left hand. Only by ramming her mutilated fist between her breasts could she stem the flow of blood. As Eagle Feather watched, she slipped to the ground, crying out her dead husband's name, her fingerless hand pulsing blood steadily into the thirsty ground.

Meanwhile, those women suffering no such immediate loss dashed to the side of the two bluecoats being dragged into the village. The two men had been made to run behind the ponies of their captors, and now, more dead than alive, they were cut loose and given over to the women. But the two soldiers were a poor catch and did little credit to the warriors who had taken them. Their spirits already broken, their scalps gone, caked blood covering their head and chests, they cowered and whimpered in terror as the band's squaws closed on them. Uttering bloodcurdling shrieks, the women stripped off the men's uniforms, the task occasioning much lunging and kicking as only the toughest, most determined of the squaws managed to make off with the highly prized jackets. One woman, one ear almost completely torn off in the struggle, pulled free triumphantly, clutching a pair of boots for her husband.

Once the men were completely naked, the women began slashing at their maggot-pale bodies, some using willow switches, others branches, and still others bringing out their pots and pans. One old fury had a heavy rifle barrel in her hand. Eagle Feather could only marvel at the strength she exhibited as she lifted it over her head and brought it down repeatedly on the two soldiers. He could hear the white-eyes' bones snapping under her repeated blows. Another old crone had somehow managed to snip off with a pair of sheers a set of the white-eyes' testicles and she was strutting about proudly, displaying the gruesome trophy to the delighted onlookers, cackling fiercely all the while.

Meanwhile, other women eagerly fed two fires. Before long, crude tripods were being erected over the leaping flames. Soon, Eagle Feather realized, the screams of these two white-eyes would fill the air as they were hung head-down, still alive, over the soaring flames.

Turning away from the women's caterwauling and shrieking—and also the cries of the soulless white men—Eagle Feather threaded his way through the village to Lame Buffalo's lodge. Pushing aside the tent flap, he stepped inside and found the old chief sitting cross-legged before his hearth, his arms folded, an impenetrable scowl on his face.

Lame Buffalo did not look up as Eagle Feather squatted on the other side of the hearth, but kept his gaze on the glowing embers before him. Out of respect for his host, Eagle Feather kept his silence. For close to half an hour they sat, one gazing into the dying embers of his lodge fire, the other waiting patiently. Abruptly, so abruptly that it startled Eagle Feather, Lame Buffalo got to his feet. He did not glance to the right or to the left as he ducked his head and stepped out through the entrance. It was as if Eagle Feather had never entered the lodge. As soon as Lame Buffalo left, a war chief entered the lodge. Eagle Feather knew him as Shakes-His-Lance. The war chief glowered down at Eagle Feather.

"The chiefs' council is meeting now," he said. "Come."

Eagle Feather got to his feet and followed Shakes-His-Lance from the tepee.

It was Shakes-His-Lance who spoke first, and he took almost an hour, pausing interminably as he spoke, for there were times when his words could not match the thoughts that rushed through his old mind. Shakes-His-Lance was a fearsomely long-winded orator, but in keeping with time-honored custom, not a single chief or warrior interrupted him. When at last he was done, he pulled his formal council robe about him and sat back down—well pleased with himself.

All he had said, over and over, was that the expedition to take only five white-eyes had been a shameful failure and that the blame for this must lie at the foot of the war party's leader, White Fox.

The first chief to speak in defense of the dead warrior was Chief Red Bear. He spoke out loudly, his voice high, like a woman's. He pointed out that this entire expedition had been Eagle Feather's idea. Not only that, but Eagle Feather had hung back during the first Blackfoot assault, content to watch from a distance while others led the charge across the stream. Only when Big Shoulders reached the canyon safely did Eagle Feather dare to take after him.

Red Bear turned to face Eagle Feather—a shocking

breach of custom—and demanded, "What do you have to say to that, Eagle Feather?"

Eagle Feather got slowly, calmly to his feet, his gaze never wavering from Red Bear's accusing gaze. He told himself he must speak with caution, but even so, he was startled at the cold fury in his voice when he spoke.

"It is not this lone Blackfoot who must be blamed for today's defeat. Why did White Fox wait until Big Shoulders and his party left the canyon? Eagle Feather watched from a distance so as not to steal any of the glory from his Blackfoot brothers. Only when he saw how badly things were going did he join the battle. It was Eagle Feather who scaled the canyon rim alongside his Gray Lodge brothers. It was he who saw Big Shoulders disappearing into the valley beyond. It is White Fox and the warriors of this band who must take the blame for this day's failure."

The oldest war chief in the band, Full Kettle, indicated that he would speak. Eagle Feather sat down. Full Kettle got to his feet. "The lone Blackfoot who has returned from the white man's land should watch his tongue," he said. "This band has never violated the laws of hospitality. But it would be wise for him to remember that this day he has brought great sorrow to many Blackfoot lodges. Let my words be a warning to him."

Eagle Feather understood now what this enfeebled Blackfoot band would now decide. So great had been their disaster this day, they could not accept it—not unless they could somehow blame it on Eagle Feather. He was, after all, in many ways a stranger to the Gray Lodge people. It was a bitter turn in Eagle Feather's fortune, for he realized now that his position among this band was now worse than precarious. All that could save him was boldness and courage.

"Eagle Feather would speak," he said.

They watched him and waited, their faces stony.

"Speak, then," said Lame Buffalo.

"You are old women," Eagle Feather told them scornfully. "You shrink from shadows. This day's disaster is your fault, and the fault of your dead war chief, White Fox. But I say no more of that now. This lone Blackfoot warrior came to the Gray Lodge band to help it regain its *puha*. But the people of the Gray Lodge have lost that chance." He paused then and let his gaze sweep around the circle of chiefs. "I leave you now. I go as I came to you, a lone Blackfoot with hate in his heart for all the white-eyes who are getting ready even now to take our land and debauch our people. I have spoken."

Eagle Feather turned and strode from the lodge.

As he walked through the village on his way to his pony, he made every effort to keep his pace unhurried. Approaching the fires where the squaws were roasting the soldiers, he made himself pause a moment to watch. The white-eyes were hanging headdown over the flames, their arms dangling loosely from their sockets, their bared skulls blackened and cracked from the intense heat, their eyes charred coals in blistered sockets. One of the white-eyes was clearly dead, but the other, incredibly, was still alive, and as he screamed, he tried to lift his head away from the flames. Every time he did so, the women would rush forward to poke him with sharpened sticks, cackling with each swift thrust. Two of them were wearing the soldier's bright-blue tunics, the highly prized brass buttons already ripped off and stored away.

Eagle Feather forced himself to resume his unhurried walk to his pony. Reaching it, he checked his war bag and rifle carefully, then mounted up. As he did so, he allowed himself one quick glance back at the village and saw the lodges and household goods of the dead warriors still being looted by the more fortunate members of the band while the grieving kin looked on like soulless hulks.

As Eagle Feather urged his mount out of the village, he was relieved to hear his spirit helper whispering in his ear, and he lifted his braid eagerly so as to catch each word: "For this unworthy Blackfoot band the shame of this day's defeat is like a stone in its throat. Do not tarry. Travel far this day."

Pleased that his spirit helper had not deserted him, Eagle Feather crouched over his pony's neck like the lobo wolf he emulated and urged it to a lope. Soon he was out of the village, and without another glance back at the lodges—for such a backward glance could reveal only weakness—he splashed across a shallow stream and entered the pine forest beyond. Once in their cover, he lifted his pony to a gallop, turning it in the direction of that valley into which he had seen Big Shoulders and the girl disappear.

As he rode, he felt elation building within him

once again. For with his spirit friend once more on hand to guide him, his magic was powerful enough to defeat all his enemies.

Including Big Shoulders.

4

The grizzly reared up onto its hind legs. A mature male, it stood at least eight feet tall. It was close to fifty yards below them on the slope, and as it looked them over, it tipped its head slightly to one side.

Kersten, terrified, could only stare back while Canyon centered the Henry's sights on the bear's chest. He didn't want to shoot it. The sound of the rifle's crack would reveal his position to any Blackfoot warriors still pursuing them. Besides, he doubted the Henry had the stopping power to hold this big bruin.

"Stay quiet. Don't move," he told Kersten softly.

She nodded dumbly, and he realized she had not needed the warning. She was already too terrified to do anything but remain frozen where she was. The grizzly finished its inspection of them and lifted its nose to test the wind. Luckily, they were downwind of the big fellow and their human scent did not reach it.

Canyon waited.

As long as the bear remained in this upright stance, he was not dangerous. But once he crashed down onto all fours and charged, his coming would be swift and deadly. One round would barely slow the beast, but he said nothing of this to Kersten. Abruptly, farther down the slope behind the grizzly, a mother and two cubs shambled into view. The big fellow caught the female grizzly's scent, whirled, dropped onto all fours, and with a thunderous *whoof* took after the mother and cubs.

Canyon knew the big fellow was in for a mean battle with the female if he tried to mess with her or the cubs, but that was not Canyon's concern as he lowered the Henry and, taking Kersten's hand, pushed on through the pines toward the distant ridge and the pass he glimpsed beyond it.

"Please," Kersten murmured after a while. "Can't we rest awhile?"

"We'll rest when it gets dark."

"No! Now! I can't go on." She yanked her hand out of his and collapsed onto the ground, her head hanging.

He halted and studied her. They had been going steadily since they left the Blackfoot behind and Kersten was close to total exhaustion. He realized wearily that it would do no good for him to bully her. She had no more reserves left.

Shifting the Henry to his left hand, he reached down and hauled her upright. Before she could protest, he flung her over his right shoulder and pushed on.

Canyon glanced across the stream at the high ground beyond, his eyes searching the undergrowth. A moment before, a movement in that thick brush had alerted him, and without a word of warning to Kersten, he had ducked into a thick stand of bullberry bushes, dragging her in after him. So far, he had seen nothing solid, only shifting shadows.

But that didn't mean a thing.

For Canyon, every foot of ground within his sight, every sound within his hearing was crammed full of the knowledge of what had happened there not long before, as well as an indication of what might come. All his senses were reaching out to gather and weigh every sign, no matter how insignificant. He could look at a squadron of ducks swimming down a stream and know without thinking whether they were looking for food or had been frightened off by a disturbance upstream. He could note the way antelope ran and tell if they were moving naturally or fleeing hunters. When he saw a branch floating in a stream, he knew whether it had fallen in through a rainstorm or other natural process or been broken off and kicked into the stream by a passing hunter. The chattering of birds could alert him to enemies, as could a disturbed bush or a browsing deer suddenly lifting its head.

So now, all senses alert, he waited.

It was two days after their confrontation with the grizzly, but he had no reason to believe he was not still being tracked by that Blackfoot band. This had made him unwilling to reveal their presence with a rifle shot or a camp fire. As a result, he had not brought down any fresh game and the two of them had not been eating well, their diet consisting for the most part of berries and those few edible roots he was able to dig out of stream banks. Kersten had balked at most of this diet. The day before, while he dined on a small family of crickets he had snatched out of a grass clump, Kersten had almost gotten sick watching him.

Close beside him now, she moved impatiently. "Canyon," she asked wearily, "What are we doing in these brambles? Can't we move on?"

"Stay still!"

"But why?"

"Never mind why, dammit, just do as I say."

"I won't!" Kersten started to get up.

Canyon yanked her closer and clamped his hand over her mouth. She tried to peel away his hand, and for a moment Canyon considered knocking her out with a single, measured blow to the chin. When she saw the grim calculation in his eyes, however, she quieted abruptly.

He looked back across the stream. What had alerted him earlier was the quick scold of a chipmunk, followed by a sudden, hushed silence, the silence of a pine forest when every articulate living thing within it crouches to watch intruders pass. The call of a mountain lark came to Canyon then, but from a long echoing distance away.

Which meant the danger was close by.

Canyon pulled back his revolver's hammer. A moment later the soft, steady pat of moccasined feet came to him. He reached out and closed his hand over Kersten's mouth. When she heard the footfalls herself now, her eyes widened in fear.

He let his hand drop from her mouth then, and keeping low, he left the cover of the bushes and cut swiftly across a small clearing, then pressed on through a thick patch of underbrush. As he moved forward, he kept to a crouch, ready to meet head-on what he assumed was an oncoming Blackfoot warrior. A twig snapped just in front of him. He held up and waited. A moment later, he glimpsed movement—man-sized—through a thick screen of brush less than three feet in front of him. He raised his revolver. Branches sprang apart and a welcome, familiar head poked through, the man's chin no more than a few inches from the bore of Canyon's revolver.

"Sam," Canyon cried. "What the hell!"

"Mind putting that cannon to one side?" Sam Wilder asked, rocking back in surprise.

At once Canyon holstered the revolver.

"Ready for me, were you?" Sam asked sheepishly.

"You're damn right. You made more commotion than a revolution."

Sam blushed. "Must be gettin' old. Anyway, this child's glad you waited before pullin' that trigger."

"You mind telling me what you're doing out here?"

"Why, hoss, I come lookin' for you."

"How'd you know I was here?"

"Easy enough. I knew sure as mothers got tits that you'd never let them Blackfoot devils take you down."

"They came close enough. What're you doing afoot?"

"Left my hoss back a ways. I could smell someone coming up this ridge." Sam sobered then and peered past Canyon. "Where's the rest?"

"Kersten's back there."

"And them two soldiers?"

"Gone, Sam."

Sam shook his head in regret. "Myself, I didn't

wait to count, Canyon. How many Blackfoot d'you suppose was in that blamed war party?''

''Not over ten. I did for four of them. It was a fine shoot, and I'm sorry you didn't stay to watch. But now I'm afoot and Kersten sure is no traveler.''

''You'll be resting up soon,'' Sam told him. ''I found me a friendly band of Nez Percé.''

''Friendly? You sure of that?''

''Sure. My woman Mountain Lamb's got kin married high up in this band, which puts me in pretty good with their chief.''

''How far's the village?'' Canyon asked.

''About five miles.''

The agent frowned. ''I'm not sure Kersten can make it that far,'' he said. ''She's done in. We haven't been eating so well, and I wouldn't let her take much time to sleep. I've been carrying her for most of yesterday and all of today.''

''Well, let's go see,'' Sam said.

They found Kersten still crouched in the bullberry bushes where Canyon had left her. When she saw them coming, she struggled upright, holding on to a tree to keep steady. Sam took one look at her and whistled softly. Seeing her in Sam's eyes, Canyon understood his surprise. Kersten's blond hair was a matted tangle of leaves and pine needles, her skirt was in tatters, and her blouse, ripped in several places, hung loosely off her bare, lacerated shoulders. In addition, her knees and legs were bloody from the branches and thorn bushes Canyon had been forced to drag her through. At the moment, she bore hardly any resemblance at all to that well-groomed, imperious young beauty who had left the fort with them such a short while ago.

Peering dazedly at Sam, she attempted a smile, but it was a wan, forlorn effort at best.

Canyon said, "Kersten, look who came back after us."

"It's . . . so nice to see you again, Sam," she told him dazedly. "I'm so glad the Indians didn't overtake you."

"We got friends near by, Miss Kersten," he assured her eagerly. "Nice friendly Nez Percé Indians with a pine-bough bed all waitin' for you. You'll be as fit as a tiger in no time."

"Look there, hoss," said Sam, halting. "Ain't that what you been looking for?"

Canyon pulled Sam's horse to a halt and followed his gaze as Wilder pointed to the valley's entrance ten miles distant. A long wagon train was snaking through it into the valley. Canyon counted almost twenty wagons in all.

That wagon train was what he had been looking for, all right. He had finally overtaken it. He was deeply grateful for this good luck, coming as it did after so much bad luck.

Sam helped Canyon lift the slumping Kersten off the horse. They carried her over to the shade of a tall pine and set her gently down. Wilder had been walking ahead with Canyon in the saddle holding on to the exhausted woman to keep her from slipping off. As she rested back on the ground, she muttered something unintelligible, but did not open her eyes. Her cheeks were flushed; Canyon was not certain, but he thought she might be running a fever.

They left her and walked a short distance up onto a small knoll, giving them an unobstructed view of the valley floor below them. Peering down at the wagons, Sam shook his head gloomily.

"Dogged if them wagon trains don't get longer every year."

"They're heading for the Promised Land, Sam."

"That's the way they see it, sure enough." Sam shook his head unhappily. "The Nez Percé don't like none of this, hoss. All these wagons scare away the game."

"How's that, Sam?"

"Well, if they'd only go on through swift and quiet, it might not be so bad. But every night these danged settlers circle their wagons, build giant bonfires, and send out packs of loud-mouthed hunters to tramp around crashing through the underbrush, looking for game they've already scattered into the next country."

Listening to Sam, Canyon realized for the first time how a full-blown wagon train must appear to the Indians and to mountain men such as Sam Wilder.

"It ain't just them settlers chasing away the game," Sam went on. "It's the infernal, riotous commotion they create. Bawling young 'uns, lowing cattle, shrill girls and their beaux rushing about at night, the stomping and clapping of their square-dancin'. Their squeakin' fiddles. But that ain't the end of it, hoss. Commencing at dawn and continuing all through the day, the ungodly racket they make as they follow the trail, their whips cracking to keep the oxen moving, the wagons creaking, the women calling back and forth as they walk beside the wagons, and then the constant shouts of the men on horseback ridin' up and down the line of wagons."

"Doesn't sound so good, at that," Canyon remarked, somewhat astonished at how garrulous his usually taciturn friend had become, aware too of just how much of a crime Sam believed this brutal, unthinking affront to the wilderness was.

"Let's go, hoss," Sam said, moving back off the knoll. "More'n likely, this wagon train'll be stoppin' close by Stalking Bear's village. There'll be some hell-raising and tradin' to do when it does." He sighed. "It'll be a goddamned circus, for sure."

When they reached Kersten, they found her fully awake, her back against the pine.

"How do you feel?" Canyon asked as he pulled her upright.

"Terrible. How far do we still have to go?"

Canyon looked questioningly at Sam.

"Just over the next hill," Sam replied.

"God," Kersten muttered bitterly, brushing an unruly lock of hair off her forehead. "Seems like that's all I've been hearing for days."

Canyon helped her move toward the horse. She managed to stay upright for a few steps, then swayed shakily. Canyon caught her in his arms. It was Sam's turn to ride. He mounted up and Canyon handed Kersten up to him. He set her down on the pommel gently and let her rest her head back against his chest.

"I'll go ahead, hoss," he told Canyon. "I want to reach the village before them blamed pilgrims do."

"Never mind me. I can keep up."

And he did.

Packs of naked children, dogs, curious warriors, and their wives trooped alongside them as they entered the Nez Percé village. Kersten was still up on the horse with Sam, her head resting back against his chest. A few of the more curious children reached up to pluck at her blond hair as it hung down.

Chief Stalking Bear strode out to greet them. The chief's broad, wrinkled face showed a subtle but definite pleasure at seeing Sam Wilder return safely, and it was clear as he gazed on Canyon that he approved of the agent's tall, broad-shouldered figure. The chief was resplendent in his finest eagle war bonnet and buckskin shirt and pantaloons. The delicate, tinkling sound of tiny bells sewn into his garment gave the chief's approach a pleasing and musical aspect.

Sam dismounted and Canyon lifted Kersten down and kept her upright as Wilder handled the formal introduction to the Nez Percé chief. To Canyon's surprise, the chief spoke excellent English and greeted Canyon with great courtesy. Meanwhile, Stalking Bear seemed filled with concern as he regarded the bedraggled and weary blonde slumped against Canyon. He asked if this was his woman.

"No, Chief. She isn't my woman. But we've been afoot for two days now. She's plumb tuckered out and needs food and rest."

"If she is not well, my women will take care of her." He turned and said something to a small boy standing close behind him.

The boy dashed off so quickly, he might have been stung by a bee.

"I'm all right," Kersten murmured. "All I need is a chance to rest up some."

Led by the small boy, the chief's two wives and

some other women came bustling up. With a sigh of relief, Kersten let herself be led away by them. This matter taken care of, the chief invited Canyon and Sam into his lodge for a smoke and some gossip. Once inside the lodge, Stalking Bear took down his ceremonial pipe, tamped in the fragrant tobacco, lit it, took a few puffs, and passed it around. As Canyon took his turn, he heard the other Nez Percé chiefs and warriors crowding close upon Stalking Bear's lodge, hoping for a glimpse of the two white visitors when they emerged.

Sam Wilder was quick to tell Stalking Bear that Canyon had accounted for four of the Blackfoot war party.

The chief looked at Canyon. "Such a killer of Blackfoot must be wary. The Blackfoot do not forget their enemies."

"I'll watch my backside, Chief," Canyon said.

"Chief," said Sam, "we saw a wagon train headin' this way."

"Stalking Bear knows of its coming. Already our people are preparing to trade pelts for those goods the settlers carry—and soon the white settlers' fiddles will kill the night's silence." He puffed a moment on his pipe, his dark, luminous eyes sad. "And when they leave, their shit will stink in the grass. It is a great trouble for our people, but they think only of the goods they will acquire and do not see it as I do."

"Maybe you should not let them through your lands anymore," Canyon suggested mischievously, knowing how difficult it would be for the Nez Percé to close off these high passes.

"I think so myself at times," Stalking Bear

agreed. He drew solemnly on his pipe for a moment longer, then handed it on to Sam. "But how can this be done? In the beginning only a few white men came, and the Nez Percé welcomed them. For the furs of the animals we kill—as plentiful as the leaves on the trees—they exchange that which the white man makes in his magic forges: iron kettles, knives, arrowheads, guns, hatchets with edges that never grow dull. But now I think we have enough kettles and knives and guns, but too many white settlers."

"Amen to that," Sam said solemnly.

For a quiet, contemplative stretch, the three men passed the pipe around, taking full lungfuls, savoring the smoke, filling the lodge with the tobacco's fragrance—this particular tobacco blend itself another wondrous gift brought to the Nez Percé by the settlers and the mountain men like Sam who passed through the Indians' lands.

Later that day, as Canyon O'Grady emerged from his bath in the stream bordering the village, he heard a commotion. Dressing quickly, he hurried back, heading for Stalking Bear's lodge, where a large crowd of villagers had already gathered.

On the way, Sam joined him. Wilder had been visiting some Indian women, one of whom—a dark, fulsome wench—trailed him now. Greeting Canyon, Sam seemed in excellent spirits. Canyon himself was feeling considerably better after his dip in the icy mountain stream.

Working their way through the crowd of braves and curious women and children closing around Stalking Bear, Canyon and Sam soon understood what was causing the commotion. The brave now speaking excitedly to Stalking Bear and the other chiefs crowding around him had just returned from scouting the approaching wagon train. As he had neared the wagons, he had spotted buzzards drifting above the trail behind the wagons. He circled behind the wagon train and came at it from the rear. From a slope above it, he witnessed three burial parties burying more than one body in hastily dug graves. So hasty were they that they had only partially covered the dead bodies.

Judging from such behavior and later from the unpleasant stench that came from the wagons when he stole closer to them, the Nez Percé scout realized what this meant: these settlers heading toward them carried in their wagons not only trade goods and fiddlers and white women in fancy dresses, but a dreadful malady, cholera.

This news stunned the Indians. They now faced an awesome dilemma.

They were eager to trade with the settlers, but that meant letting the settlers make camp close by their village. Soon the Indians would be sharing the settlers' jugs of firewater as they bartered. In short, it meant the Nez Percé were about to join in a close, intimate association with a people who brought with them a miserable, unclean death. This aching curse of the bowels would soon flush their life's fluids from them in an agonizing, putrescent stream, turning its victim into a pitiable wreck in the space of one day, making it unlikely even that he would survive the night.

Arms folded, Stalking Bear listened to the suggestions that flew at him from his chiefs. Some were for driving the wagons way. Others wanted to stop them at what they considered was a safe distance from the village and allow the settlers and Nez Percé to trade if they wanted.

Others, however, wanted only to flee, to strike their lodgepoles and slip away before this white man's curse overtook them. Those who suggested this, Canyon noted, were the older chiefs, those who had probably visited white settlements or forts in the past and had seen what devastation cholera could visit on a people.

With Sam at his side, Canyon strode quietly toward the chief and paused beside him. Stalking Bear saw that Canyon wanted to speak and at once the chief introduced him.

When he had finished doing so, Canyon raised his hand. "Hear me," he said. "I know what a terrible curse is this cholera. So terrible is it, I would tell you to strike your lodges and flee this valley if I knew of no other way to deal with it."

There were a few mutters of agreement to this, and the older chiefs nodded their heads approvingly.

Canyon continued. "But there is another way. Let me and Sam speak to the leader of this wagon train. We will stop it from coming closer. We will keep the settlers away from the Nez Percé and prevent any trading of goods. Only when the sickness is gone from these wagons will we allow the wagons to continue on through the valley."

There was a quick mutter of agreement to this plan, though some were not so pleased, thinking it not drastic enough. These chiefs glanced at Stalking Bear to get his reaction to Canyon's proposal.

Stalking Bear's response came instantly.

"Canyon's plan is good," he said, his eyes moving about the crowd. "He will stop the wagons. No Nez Percé will trade with these settlers. When the stinking sickness is gone from them, the Nez Percé will let them pass. If any Indian from this village trades with these settlers, he will be cast out of this band forever. And if any Nez Percé brings a settler to this village, both will be killed. I have spoken. If any chief wishes to disagree with me in this, let him speak now."

For a moment it appeared that one or two chiefs were about to step forward and object, but the weight of opinion was so heavily in favor of the plan that they thought better of it and did not protest. Satisfied that Canyon's plan and his own endorsement of it had carried, Stalking Bear turned to Canyon, his eyes shining with gratitude.

"Keep this pestilence away from my people and you will do us a great service, Canyon. You will not go unrewarded. That I promise."

"Thanks, Chief."

"When will you start?"

"As soon as Sam and I can get our gear together." He looked at Sam. "Right, Sam?"

Sam nodded.

"And I'll need a horse."

"Canyon will have mine," said the chief.

Before Canyon rode out, he visited the sick lodge where Kersten was being taken care of by Stalking Bear's women. He found them fussing about her like worker bees over their queen. The women had thrown away Kersten's skirt and blouse and dressed her in a doeskin shift, then washed her hair. Over the scratches on her arms and legs they'd slapped gobs of bear grease, and when Canyon rode up, he saw a sweat lodge being prepared for her.

She had a persistent fever, the women indicated to him, and it was going to be necessary for her to sweat it out in the lodge. When Canyon tried to point out that what she really needed was a good meal, they just laughed at him. Exasperated, he chased the women out of the lodge.

"How do you feel now?" he asked Kersten.

"Weak. So damn weak. Canyon, will I ever get my strength back?"

"You need food, dammit!"

"I know."

Canyon went to the lodge entrance and called over an old woman and in no uncertain terms told her he wanted hot broth to be brought to Kersten. When the old crone hesitated, he told her that if she did not provide this broth for Kersten before she entered the sweat lodge, he would come back as the Great Cannibal Owl and carry her off to his nest high in the mountains and there devour her liver.

This preposterous threat was enough. With a mournful cry, the old woman hurried off to do Canyon's bidding.

"What on earth did you tell that poor old woman?" Kersten asked him.

"Sam's been telling me some wild Indian stories, so I dressed one up and used it to scare her into bringing you some broth."

"How ever can I thank you?"

"Get well. That'll be thanks enough."

"You were so terrible to me . . . out there."

"I had to be."

"I know. I understand that now."

He got to his feet. "I'm moving out now. Won't be seeing you for a while."

"Where are you going?"

"There's a wagon train with cholera on its way. Sam and I are going to stop it before it gets any closer to the village."

"Cholera! Oh, my God. Be careful."

"I promise you I will." He bent then and kissed her lightly on her pale lips, then left. As he swung into his saddle, he caught sight of the old squaw hurrying toward the sick lodge, holding a huge bowl of steaming broth.

He chuckled. Now, if only he and Sam could handle this business with the settlers as easily . . .

"You mind telling me why you was so quick to count me in on this?" Sam asked.

They were on their way out of the village, heading for the wagon train. Since they planned on a long stay while they kept the wagons in place, they were leading two heavily laden packhorses.

Canyon grinned at him. "I thought for sure you'd want to come along, Sam. I know how you like fiddle music."

"That ain't the kind of music we're likely to hear. More like wailin' and callin' upon the Lord to deliver 'em. Tell me, Canyon, since you got all the answers. How're we goin' to keep getting this here cholera ourselves?"

"First off, we're not going near the wagons. Soon as we smell it—and that won't be hard—we'll pull up and wait for the wagon master to ride out to meet us."

"Suppose he's got it?"

"If he's got it, he won't be riding any horse. Besides, we won't let him get close. We'll keep him a good distance from us when we talk."

"Then, what?"

"We let the contagion burn itself out."

"What you're doin' is quarantining them."

"That's right, Sam."

"And you're also getting a line on that gent you come after."

"That too, Sam."

Wilder had no more comment and the two men rode on in silence. The Indian scout had told them that the wagon train was at least five miles farther down the valley and they settled into a steady, ground-devouring lope. The sooner they stopped the wagons, the better. Every mile closer it got to the Nez Percé village increased the danger to the Indians.

During a trip to Boston a few years back Canyon had overheard the captains of those great merchant ships talk of cholera epidemics they had witnessed in the Far Eastern ports they had put into. It was these seafaring men's considered opinion that the burning of corpses and strict, personal cleanliness was the only sure protection against the scourge—that and a quarantine.

Now, if these settlers were willing to take his direction, Canyon would suggest they follow that advice. Out here in the wilderness achieving a state of strict cleanliness would not be all that easy. But since no one had the slightest notion what caused this hellish plague, what other course had they?

And if the settlers ignored his suggestions and insisted on keeping on through the valley to trade with the Nez Percé, Canyon knew what he and Sam had to do. After all, they had promised Chief Stalking Bear.

It was a promise Canyon would keep.

5

As Canyon had suspected, they were able to smell the wagon train before they reached it.

Canyon reined in the chief's appaloosa and glanced at a very unhappy Sam Wilder. Sam's sense of smell was every bit as keen as Canyon's.

"You can go back if you want, Sam."

"We come this far, Canyon."

They rode on and a few minutes later topped a rise and saw on the flat before them, less than half a mile distant, the first of the wagons. It was a mite ahead of the others, the rest strung out in ragged fashion. It had the look of a sick train, all right. A mile or so to the north, the stream that wound past the Nez Percé village farther west came in sight, flanked by cottonwood and aspen. One look at the stream with the timber shading it gave Canyon some hope that his plan might work.

He booted his pony down the gentle slope and headed toward the lead wagon. He had not gone far when a rider appeared and whipped his horse toward them. Canyon reined in, snaked his Henry out of its sling, cranked a fresh round into its firing chamber, and waited calmly. When the rider got within hailing distance, Canyon lifted his weapon and sent a round over his head.

The man pulled up, confused and angry.

"You the wagon master?" Canyon shouted.

"That's right," the man yelled back. "You sure ain't very friendly, mister, shootin' at me like that."

"Just a warning shot so you'd keep your distance. It was well over your head. What's your name?"

"Brewster. I'm deacon of the All Souls Baptist Church out of Glenbrook, Ohio. Who might you be?"

"Canyon O'Grady. This man beside me is Sam Wilder."

Deacon Brewster was a gray-bearded man in his late forties, a narrow, spindly fellow with squinting eyes and a mean, down-turned mouth. He looked more like an undertaker than a pioneer. His floppy brimmed hat, coat, trousers, and boots were all black. Only his shirt was white broadcloth, and that was soiled enough to match the rest of his garb.

"We heard you got the cholera," Sam Wilder said.

"Yes. And we need help. There's an Indian village up ahead, where we intend to trade for fresh meat. We'll need that to get our health back."

"You can forget that village, Brewster," Canyon told him. "Your wagons won't be going any farther, and you won't be getting any fresh meat from the Indians."

"What do you mean, O'Grady? You can't stop this wagon train."

"Sure we can. One at a time, if that's what it takes."

"This here ain't your land."

"Well, it sure as hell ain't yours, mister," Sam snapped.

A second rider had already left the wagon train, and when Brewster heard his hoofbeats, he glanced back. Seeing who it was, he waited for the rider to join him. This newcomer, Canyon noticed, was younger, clean-shaven, and looked a mite more agreeable than the stern-faced deacon of the All Souls Baptist Church. As soon as Brewster had explained the situation to the younger man, he leaned back in his saddle and peered curiously at Canyon and Sam, a frown on his face.

"Is what Deacon Brewster tells me correct? Do you actually mean to stop our wagon train from moving on?"

"For now, yes," Canyon replied. "And who might you be?"

"I've been elected by the members of the wagon train to serve as second-in-command to Deacon Brewster. My name's MacDonald."

What that meant, Canyon knew at once, was that these unhappy settlers had recently had a rump election and put MacDonald in charge, effectively removing the wagon train from the Deacon Brewster's control. As a sop to the deacon the settlers had let him keep his title as wagon master.

Canyon pointed to the cottonwoods bordering the distant stream. "I'm suggesting your wagon train halt over by the stream in among them cottonwoods. Stay there until the cholera burns itself out—no matter how long it takes. And later, when you pass on through the valley, keep well away from the Nez Percé village."

"You must be out of your head, Canyon. We can't

do that. We need to trade with the Nez Percé for fresh food and meat. It could go far toward helping us recover.''

''Maybe so, but you don't know that for a fact. What is a fact is you would bring cholera into the village—and maybe wipe out every Nez Percé in it.''

MacDonald nodded slowly. ''Yes, of course. I see what you mean.''

''One more thing.''

''What's that?''

''We could smell your train before we crested the hill behind us. I suggest you start cleaning yourselves up. Take baths in that stream over there. Scrub yourselves. Boil your clothes and your bedding. Boil the water you drink. Bury your dead a good distance from the stream. And each wagon should dig a deep hole for its night soil—as deep a hole as can be dug.''

''Are you some kind of doctor?''

''I'm no doctor. But from what I know of cholera, it likes crowded, dirty places where people live close enough together to foul their nests. Maybe if you spread your wagons out and cleaned yourselves up some, the cholera would die out. It's only a chance, and not much of one, at that. But right now, it's the only one I'm giving you.''

MacDonald considered Canyon's words, then he turned in his saddle and shaded his eyes as he studied the distant cottonwoods and the stream beyond. Then, with a fatalistic shrug, he turned back around in his saddle and looked at the deacon. ''I don't think we got much choice, Brewster. I say we do what this fellow suggests.''

''You mean let them stop us?''

''It's the cholera that's stopping us, not them.''

"I won't have it."

"Go ahead and argue with these two if you want. I'm not going to bother."

"But this is outlawry," the deacon insisted, "plain and simple."

MacDonald looked past Brewster at Canyon and Sam. "Deal with Brewster here as you will. I'm going back to turn the wagons into those cottonwoods." He pulled his horse around and rode back to the wagon train.

Fuming, the deacon sat his horse a moment, staring at Canyon and Sam as if his gaze alone would be enough to turn them to stone. At last, fairly bursting with indignation, he tugged his horse around and followed after MacDonald. Before he reached the wagon train, MacDonald had already sent the lead wagon toward the stream, and the rest were following.

"Them two gents—the deacon and MacDonald—are goin' to tangle, I'm thinking," Sam commented.

"When they do, I'll be betting on MacDonald."

"Me, too."

"Now all we have to do, Sam, is keep the settlers and the Nez Percé apart. And make camp on ground high enough to give us a good view of things."

"I already found the spot."

"Where?"

"Over there," he said, pointing to a knoll that overlooked the stream and the cottonwoods less than a quarter-mile farther on.

"Yep. That'll do fine," Canyon said, turning his pony.

As he and Sam made for the knoll, the U.S. agent wondered about Judge Langley and that bodyguard of his, Jake Gettis. There was a chance they might already have succumbed to cholera. He would like to have asked MacDonald if Langley was on the train, but had he done so, it would have been a dead giveaway. Out here in the wilderness, thousands of miles from Cincinnati, a rider showing up asking for Judge Fowler G. Langley would have given the judge all the warning he needed.

Meanwhile, Canyon had no desire to visit the wagon train and seek out Langley himself, which meant he would just have to keep his eyes and his options open. The thing was, he still did not know precisely how—when the time came—he was going to deal with Judge Langley, the man who had already tried once to assassinate a president.

As Canyon and Sam had expected, the settlers' first attempt to make it through to the Indian village came at dusk. Far below them on the flat two women and six men carrying rifles appeared, the women pushing a four-wheeled barrow piled high with trade goods. Canyon and Sam mounted up and rode down off the knoll to cut them off, splitting up before they reached the settlers in order to come upon them from two directions.

Canyon rode directly at them from the front. His pony's hooves muffled by the thick grass, he appeared before them out of the gathering dusk, his surprise complete. As he rode closer, the settlers cowered back. Only one of the men had enough sand to lift his rifle, but as he did so, Sam materialized out of the gloom beside him and in a low, almost confident tone advised him to lower his weapon.

The settler promptly did so.

"Get back to your wagons," Canyon told them, "or we'll blow a hole in that barrow."

"How dare you," cried one of the women, her bony hands clutching at the string of her black bonnet.

Canyon could smell them even from this distance. Like most people on the trail, they were so used to each other's stench, they no longer noticed—or cared—how rank they had become. It took someone coming upon them from the outside to notice. He wondered if there was any other animal in the world as foul-smelling as an unclean human.

"You can't stop us from going where we want," one of the men whined. "This is a free country. We got our rights."

Sam said, "So have them Indians you want to trade with."

"Didn't MacDonald tell you what I told him," Canyon said. "No one from the wagons is to trade with the Nez Percé."

"He did," the woman snapped shortly. "But he ain't our deacon, and I sure didn't vote for that MacDonald upstart, or that other one, either."

"What other one?" Canyon asked quickly.

"That Judge Langley. He says we should follow him, but we won't. It's the deacon we're following. He got us this far."

"He surely did, praise the Lord," seconded the other woman.

"How many have you already lost to the cholera?" Sam asked.

"Eight," the fellow muttered.

"Since when?"

"Last week." As the fellow spoke, he stepped toward Canyon.

A trifle hastily, Canyon pulled back his horse. "Stay back," he growled. "Keep your distance."

"Why, we's all right," said one of the other men. "Not a one of us is sick. It's them Kittles and Smarts, they's the ones always eatin' poorly cooked pork."

"You sure that's what it is, are you? Bad pork?"

"Of course," said one of the women. "What else could it be?"

"I don't know," said Canyon curtly. "And neither do you. So turn back. And tell anyone else who wants to trade with the Nez Percé that the next time we'll shoot first and ask questions later."

"Hey, mister," the fellow with the rifle demanded sullenly, "just who in tarnation made you the law around here?"

Canyon patted his Henry. "This."

Sam spoke up then. "All right. That's enough palaver. Turn around and get back to them wagons. And do it now, 'cause I ain't as patient and polite as my partner."

With a few surly glances back over their shoulders at Canyon and Sam, the men waited for the women to turn the barrow around, then escorted them back across the darkening meadowland.

Canyon and Sam followed behind at a safe distance until the party reached the outskirts of the wagon train.

As the returning settlers were joined by those who had remained behind, MacDonald rode out to speak with Canyon and Sam. Canyon halted him with a raised hand while he was still a good distance away.

"What's your explanation, MacDonald?" Canyon asked him.

"I couldn't hold them back," MacDonald admitted, "not without a battle. I hoped you'd be out there."

"Tell the others that if any more try that, they won't be walking back. I'll shoot the next settler who tries to reach that Nez Percé village."

"You mean that, do you?"

"MacDonald, it's either them or the Nez Percé. I prefer the Indians. Now, are you doing what I said, separating the wagons and cleaning them and yourselves up?"

"I'll try it tomorrow."

"You got people still coming down with the cholera?"

"We have."

"Well, then, you better start tonight. The sooner the better."

"It seems like such a . . . useless thing to do."

"Suit yourself," Canyon snapped coldly. "But maybe you'll be singing a different tune when this night's done."

Canyon wheeled the appaloosa and rode off with Sam in grim silence, an angry, perplexed frown on his face. Why in hell was it such an unpleasant prospect for these settlers to clean themselves up?

When Canyon and Sam reached their camp, they found two Nez Percé women waiting for them. A packhorse leading a travois stood some distance away.

"Hoss," said Sam, winking, "I see lodgepoles on that travois. There's enough skin there for two lodges. It looks like these two young ladies is plannin' on stayin' awhile.''

"You're going to let them stay?''

"Of course. But I'll have to frighten them a little—to make them more grateful when I give in.'' Sam nudged his horse toward the two women, scowling. "What in tarnation you two doin' here?'' he demanded in mock anger as he slipped off his mount and walked up to them.

His anger was not in the least convincing, however, and the Nez Percé women simply laughed at him. One of them was the same one Canyon had seen Sam with earlier, a chunky, bright-eyed young lady whose large, glowing eyes seemed to devour Sam.

"Stalking Bear say we should come to warm your bed,'' she told Sam.

"He did, did he?'' Sam looked over at Canyon, a pleased light in his eyes. "What do you make of this, Canyon?''

Canyon shrugged. "I gather you know that one.''

"You mean Night Bird here? Hell, Canyon, she's kin to my own Shoshone woman. She figures it's her bounden duty to keep me happy till Mountain Lamb can tend to my needs herself. Ain't no harm in that.''

"I know that.''

"And this here other woman's for you. The way I figure it, the chief sent her along so you wouldn't be left out.''

"That's real thoughtful of him. What's she called?''

Sam walked over to the taller Nez Percé woman standing beside Night Bird and, taking her arm gently, escorted her over to O'Grady.

"Hoss," Sam said, "meet Fern Song. She's a Flathead, and she knew my woman when they was kids together. Fern Song came to this village a year ago when a Nez Percé warrior purchased her sister from a Flathead chief. This here woman you're lookin' at's a chief's daughter—and every inch a princess."

Canyon looked into the lovely, luminous eyes of this slender, willowy Flathead woman. Her face was round and pleasing, a hint of a cleft in her chin; she had small, delicate hands and feet and well-formed limbs. She had brushed her hair until it was glossy and hung in thick braids down upon her swelling breasts. The part line she had colored with vermilion. She had rouged her forehead, nose, and cheeks ever so faintly, and had blended herbs, grass, pine needles, and flowers into a scent with which she perfumed her body and garments.

Sam had called her a princess, and in truth no royal highness had ever been clad more regally. Her doeskin dress was beaten thin and whitened, the skirt fringed with tiny bells, the bodice decorated with colored quills and ribbons that she had fashioned into the shape of a flower. Cinched about her tiny waist was a wide leather belt, onto which she had sewn a geometric design of multicolored beads.

She smiled warmly at him and he reached out and took her small, lovely hand in his. Its warmth flowed through him, and he asked himself how long it had been since he had felt the warmth of a woman's body beside him on his couch.

Canyon looked at Sam. "Be sure and remind me to thank the chief."

When Fern Song slipped in under Canyon's blanket that night, her warm, silken limbs pressing eagerly against his, there was no reluctance on his part. He took her in his arms with a need so ferocious it surprised him. Insatiable as he, she fell upon him, her tongue probing wantonly, her warm eager body pressing urgently against his. Waiting for her, he had found himself growing eagerly. Now, pleased at his eagerness for her, she laughed softly and spread her legs, and he felt her moist pubis accepting his erection. Slipping deeper into her hot, moist warmth, he uttered an eager grunt and rolled over onto her, cleaving her effortlessly. As her tight cleft closed hungrily about his thrusting erection, he flung off all conscious volition and began thrusting wildly, deeply, feeling her clinging to him, accepting each thrust with a slight moan of pleasure.

Her hands clawed at his buttocks while her long-limbed frame rose up hungrily to meet each thrust. She began to moan constantly now, every now and then crying out something in her Nez Percé tongue that sounded suspiciously like a curse. But he paid no attention as she thrust herself recklessly, fiercely up at him, devouring his pounding erection. No longer gentle, he plunged recklessly down into her, impaling her on his fiery lance, the shock of it causing her to shudder with delight. She flung her arms around his neck. Wildly aroused, he caught her mouth with his, entwined his tongue about hers.

Her arms still wrapped about his neck, she clung to him, groaning in ecstasy, nearing her climax, her lovely face taut with the pull of it. Shuddering, she flung herself upward, arching her back. Hanging there, clinging to him, frozen in space, she climaxed, a fierce cry bursting from her lips. It sounded like the night cry of a she-cougar.

Canyon slammed down onto her, driving home with an urgency as powerful as hers—and the dam broke. In a series of powerful, involuntary ejaculations, he came and came again, emptying his seed deep within her. She clung to him, sucking him in deeper with each convulsive thrust, laughing softly, darkly. When he had finished, he rolled off her and drifted almost immediately into a drugged sleep. The last thing he remembered was her leaning over him like a great cat, her cool hands stroking his face, her soft lips laving his, her voice lulling him.

It was still night when Fern Song awoke him and he found himself on his back, her legs astride his waist as she braced herself on her arms and planted herself firmly down onto his nocturnal erection. With a deep sigh, she leaned back, taking him clear to the hilt, then began to rock back and forth, her breasts swaying gently, a nipple occasionally brushing his cheek.

When she saw him looking up at her in astonishment, she smiled, lowered her lips to his, and kissed him, her tongue probing lightly at his lips, laving them with fire. He came awake with a vengeance then, humping urgently up at her, on fire with his dreamlike need for her. Laughing softly, she released his lips and sat back on him and worked herself down still farther onto his shaft.

Faster and faster, harder and harder, she drove down upon him, her dark hair billowing as she flung her head from side to side. He was almost out of control by now, rushing to his climax, when she abruptly flung her head back and came in an explosive, shuddering spasm. As she pulsed, the muscles inside her squeezed him tight. He drove up into her, and in an explosive rush, he came, bucking wildly with each spasm.

Fern Song hung on to him and shrieked softly, coming with him again and again until she finally collapsed forward, her damp cheek resting on his powerful chest. Completely spent, lying back quietly, Fern Song's long, silken warmth covering him, Canyon stroked her hair and felt his spent organ recede gently from her moistness.

She murmured to him softly in her own tongue, leaned close, and kissed him softly on his brow; then she dropped beside him and snuggled close against him like a great cat. As he followed after her into his second delicious sleep of the night, the last thing he remembered was the gentle perfume of her breath on his cheek as she slept in the crook of his powerful arm.

Midmorning of the next day Canyon and Sam rode down to the wagons. Canyon wanted to know how the settlers had come through the night. Cholera could strike swiftly, and when a man was in the clutches of this ugly affliction, a single night could easily be long enough to take him. The U.S. agent was also hoping to catch a glimpse of the man he had come so far to find. It had not surprised him to learn the night before that Langley was leading a third contingent of restless settlers who were not altogether content with the way things were going.

Pulling up a good distance from the nearest wagon, Canyon and Sam sat their mounts and waited for the

95

wagon master or MacDonald to make his appearance. Canyon noted with some satisfaction that many of the wagons had pulled back a considerable distance from their neighbors and that other wagons were in the process of doing the same. Also, though he realized that from this distance he might be mistaken, the fetid stench that had hung over the wagons seemed to have lifted somewhat.

It was MacDonald who rode out to greet them. When he reined in, Canyon and Sam found themselves looking at a very grim young man.

"Well?" Canyon said.

"It was a bad night. We lost five more. Two went in the night, three this morning."

"What does the wagon master say to that?"

"He was one of them. Him and his oldest son. And this morning we got two more with stomach cramps."

"I see you're moving your wagons apart."

"We're doin' what you said. It's better than doing nothing. We'll keep each family as far apart as we can. No mingling. No borrowing. In addition, we'll be boiling the water we drink and everything else, bedclothes, clothing, and we'll be scrubbing down each wagon. You're right, Canyon. We stink to high heaven. Each one of us is going to scrub himself down to the bone. It may not do any good, but if we die, at least we can die clean."

"Where you buryin' the bodies?" Sam asked.

MacDonald turned in his saddle and pointed downstream. "In those hills back there—well above the stream."

"How deep are your night-soil trenches?"

"As deep as we can get them."

"See to it that everyone uses them, even those with cholera." With a nod to Sam, Canyon pulled his appaloosa around. "Good luck, MacDonald," he called over his shoulder.

"O'Grady . . . ?"

Canyon pulled up to look back.

"Could you spare us some fresh meat? We're near out."

Canyon glanced at Sam.

Sam stroked his chin thoughtfully. "Maybe we could have some braves drop fresh deer meat out here in the grass for 'em," he suggested. "They wouldn't have to get much closer than this."

Canyon glanced back at MacDonald. "We'll see what we can do."

"God be with you, O'Grady."

Canyon set his pony in motion, thinking, God better be with you, MacDonald. At this rate, there won't be much need for fresh venison.

It was a gloomy, disquieting thought.

6

A week after the quarantine of the wagon train had begun, Tim Flannery showed up.

His two packhorses laden with plews, the old mountain man was on his way out of Blackfoot territory on his way to Fort Billings. A buckskin shirt fell in large folds around his gaunt body, his buckskin leggings clinging to his skinny legs. His weapon was an ancient Hawken. He had come through Blackfoot territory because there were no more beaver left anywhere else in the Rockies. A whiff of the "death wagons," as he called them, had stopped him, and when he visited the Nez Percé, they told him what was afoot. So he showed up on the knoll, hoping to maybe pick up some fresh tobacco if Sam had any.

Sam was more than pleased to see Flannery and made him welcome, filling his stomach with buffalo meat until he had belched himself into contentment. As night fell, the three retired to a log on the crest of the knoll and let Fern Song and Night Bird build up the camp fire, around which they lit their pipes, passed around the jug of Taos Lightning Flannery happened to have with him, and set to talking.

After Canyon and Sam had explained why they

were holding up the wagon train, Old Tim allowed as how it was a good idea to stop a wagon train for any reason. As far as he was concerned, they were responsible for the present parlous state of the fur trade. He didn't make the connection any too clear as far as Canyon could make out, but that didn't matter much by then as the jug made its third round.

"What's beaver worth in Taos?" Sam asked, handing the jug back to Flannery.

"Two dollars."

"What about in St. Louis?"

"The same."

Sam shook his head in disbelief. "Any call for buckskin?"

"A heap. The soldiers in Santa Fe are half froze for leather, and moccasins fetch four dollars a pair."

"How's powder goin'?"

"Three dollars a pint."

"Tobacco?"

"Takes a plew to get one plug."

Sam shook his head and glanced at Canyon. "Looks like the only thing left to hunt will be buffalo—and them not for long, I'm thinking."

"You hear about Bridger?" Flannery asked.

"Nope," Sam replied. "What about him?"

"Can you believe he's keepin' store?"

"Maybe you better explain that."

"He's done turned Fort Bridger into a supply base for these blamed settlers, sellin' 'em horses, provisions, all kinds of supplies. As far as Jim's concerned, there's be no more trapping for him."

"Maybe he's right," Canyon said.

"This child don't see that," Flannery said.

"There's still streams ain't been mined, beaver that ain't been found."

Neither Canyon nor Sam wanted to argue the point with Flannery, and the talk drifted then to the earlier, shining times when small armies of trappers combed the mountains for beaver and came together at the spring rendezvous laden with plews. They did a good deal of combing over the hell-raising that took place during those trading sessions, recalling the battles with liquored-up Indians and outraged grizzlies, the adventures shared; and at the last of it, they spoke of all the trappers that had gone under.

Canyon listened to the two old mountain men with great interest, realizing as he did that he was a witness to a mighty adventurous time that was now pretty near done—as the settlers and surveyors swept into the western land to claim it for their own. There would soon be no room for grizzlies or the buffalo.

Or the Indians.

The Taos Lightning soon took its toll and the talk eased off. Flannery sighed and looked over at Fern Song and Night Bird, waiting patiently in front of their lodges for the men to warm their beds.

"See you got you some squaws to keep," he remarked. "Ten years back, I packed a Ute squaw along. I gave my buffalo horse and four packs of beaver for her, and she made the best moccasins I ever wore. She was rubbed out by the Cheyenne, and after she was gone under, I tried no more."

"Why's that?" Canyon asked.

"I told you. It's safer alone. Besides, a woman's breast is the hardest rock there is and leaves no trail that I can see."

Picking up the jug, Flannery took one last swallow and lurched off into the brush with his Hawken. He had been offered a spot in Sam's tepee. But as always, Flannery cached alone.

Flannery left the next morning without fanfare. After he was gone, Canyon and Sam rode down to the wagon train. As had become customary, they halted the two hundred yards or so from the nearest wagon and waited for MacDonald to show. Almost at once MacDonald was riding out to greet them.

Canyon spoke first. "Sam and I haven't seen any burial parties the last couple of days."

"There haven't been any, and that's a fact." MacDonald's voice conveyed a resonance it had formerly lacked.

"For how long exactly?"

"Three days now."

Canyon looked past him at the scattered wagons. He wasn't sure, but they appeared cleaner—and then he realized why. The white canvases they used to cover the frames had all been washed.

Canyon turned to Sam. "Let's ride a bit closer and take a look around."

With MacDonald accompanying them at a discreet distance, they rode downstream, keeping a good safe distance from each of the wagons. One of the first things Canyon noticed was the scarcity of settlers. When he remarked on this to MacDonald, the young man nodded grimly.

"We lost quite a few, I am afraid."

"How many?"

"Close to a third of our complement. We'll be leaving a few wagons behind."

"If you do, burn them."

Keeping on, Canyon noted the lines of wash flapping in the breeze and the scrubbed appearance of the wagons and of the men and women as well. He was pleased. Maybe they had licked the cholera, after all.

Maybe.

Pulling up after passing the last wagon, O'Grady said to MacDonald. "Looks like you might be all right now, MacDonald. I say give it four more days and we'll know for sure."

It was clear MacDonald was disappointed; he would have liked to gather his wagons together and move on out sooner, but he did not argue. "By the way," he said. "The settlers want me to thank you for the fresh venison the Indians have been leaving for us. It has made all the difference, I'm sure. What we haven't eaten we've dressed and are drying out for the remainder of the trip."

"Least we could do," Canyon told him. "Couldn't let you starve."

With a wave to MacDonald, Canyon and Sam rode off.

"How do you figure it, hoss?" Wilder asked as they neared their camp. "You think them damn pilgrims really got the cholera beat?"

"I don't know, Sam, but I sure as hell hope so."

"They did clean up some, I swear. You think that's what done it?"

"You know what I told MacDonald. Disease seems to take over where there's too much crowding and human filth. They cleaned themselves up and now there are no more cases of cholera. Figure it out for yourself."

"Just four more days," Sam said, glancing back at the wagons. "I'll bet they can hardly wait."

"I'm just as anxious to see them go as you are, Sam."

"Only there's a man you got to get in that wagon train somewhere, means you'll have to stay with it. How you goin' to manage that?"

"Wish I knew, Sam."

"Maybe they'll need a guide."

"I don't know this country."

"I do."

"I'm not asking you to throw in with me, Sam. This is my job. You got your own business to attend to."

"We left Fort Billings together, hoss. We might as well stick it out for a while longer."

"I'll keep that in mind, Sam. Thanks."

It was his spirit helper that awakened Eagle Feather, its abrasive tongue licking at the Blackfoot's face and eyelids, bidding him to rise and continue after Broad Shoulders.

The Indian sat up and saw the shadowy figure of the lobo wolf dart away, its tail down, then turn and look at him, tongue lolling, eyes gleaming like embers. When he tried to call out to the lobo wolf, his mouth was too dry. He could not make a sound. At last he struggled to a sitting position and looked about him, ashamed that he let himself sleep so long into the next day. His pony was not in sight, and when he looked back for the lobo wolf, it had vanished.

Eagle Feather got up and looked down the slope beside his night camp. His pony was grazing contentedly in the meadow below. He trotted down the slope, leapt astride it, and continued on with renewed hope, even though he had long since lost the spoor of the hated Big Shoulders. His spirit helper was guiding him, which meant that soon he would overtake the hated white-eyes. By the end of that day he came in sight of white, canvas-covered wagons on the other side of the stream. The wagons had been halted in a grove of cottonwoods.

He had no more bullets for his rifle. And he had no tools for fashioning a bow or for making arrows that would not tumble or veer in flight. His only weapons were his knife and war hatchet. Since he left the village of the Gray Lodge Blackfoot, he had not been very successful killing game. He had snared only one rabbit, and now his stomach contracted painfully as it came to him how close he was to fresh meat. Even this far from the wagons, he could smell the freshly killed game roasting over open fires.

That night, he promised himself, he would sneak into the wagon train and take what he wanted. Of course, he would be careful not to raise an alarm. He was alone and wished to make no new enemies.

He kept in the timber, and that night, when he visited one of the wagons most distant from the others, he found to his delight racks of drying meat and fed himself immediately. His hunger eased, he continued past the other wagons, delighting in his skill at moving through the white-eyes' encampment undetected. From one wagon he pilfered a sack of salt, from another the loin of a small antelope. Well-satisfied with his plunder, he fled back into the timber.

He fed himself the next night in the same manner, careful not to alert any of the settlers to his presence by taking too much at a time. During the day, while he watched the wagons closely, he discovered where the fresh game was coming from. Nez Percé braves were dropping recently killed antelope some distance from the wagons and the settlers were taking it back to the wagons. Why the Nez Percé should be doing this, he had no idea. Another curious thing was that the wagon train was remaining for such a long while alongside the stream without moving on.

His curiosity whetted, on the third night Eagle Feather ignored the wagon train and, circling it, headed on foot for a camp fire he saw burning on a distant knoll. Approaching it from behind through a screen of pine, he found his way blocked by two Nez Percé lodges. From inside the lodges came the sound of women making up the night's couches. He pulled back and peered through a clump of bushes at the camp fire burning in the small clearing in front of them.

What he saw then made his heart leap. He almost cried out in triumph.

Surely, Eagle Feather's magic was greater than that of any other Blackfoot.

Sitting on a log not a hatchet's flight from him was Big Shoulders. He was sitting with an old trapper, and the two of them were drinking from a jug and talking loudly, laughing often. Much of what they said was lost on Eagle Feather, but it soon became clear that these men were waiting for the wagon train to move on. This, it seemed, was why they waited in this valley.

Eagle Feather eased carefully back into the bushes.

His first instinct had been to attack Big Shoulders that same night. While he slept. But such a course would be foolhardy. There were two men here, not just one, and no matter how silently he killed, the women would wake and give an outcry that would bring the entire Nez Percé nation down upon him.

No. His spirit helper was powerful—but not all-powerful. One must not push the medicine of one's *puha* too far.

Soon, the wagon train would start up again, of this Eagle Feather was certain, for all these foolish settlers wanted was to reach the Great Water beyond these mountains. Eagle Feather did not understand why this was so, but it did not matter to him. When Big Shoulders joined the wagon train, Eagle Feather would follow and await his chance.

He would meet Big Shoulders on even terms. There would be no bungled ambush this time, and no Nez Percé to help his enemy cut Eagle Feather down.

It would be just the two of them.

Eagle Feather felt his spirit soar at the prospect.

Astride their mounts, Canyon and Sam watched the wagon train moving out below them. It was a bright morning and in the two weeks since this strange vigil had begun, summer had come to the mountains. Behind the wagon train, four abandoned wagons were burning, the flames sending a dark pillar of smoke into the sky.

The sound of muffled hoofbeats behind him caused Canyon to turn and see Stalking Bear and two other chiefs riding up to watch the wagons pull out. Earlier, before dawn, Fern Song and Night Bird had packed their travois and taken their lodges back to the village. They had wasted no time spreading the news of the wagon train's departure.

"You have done a fine thing, Canyon," Stalking Bear said. "My people are safe now."

"Maybe so, Chief," Canyon replied. "But I'll feel a whole lot better when these wagons leave this valley far behind."

The chief grunted his assent.

A familiar rider left the train and rode toward them. It was MacDonald. Canyon guessed he was coming to bid them good-bye, something he had expected.

Nudging his mount, Canyon angled down the slope to meet him, Sam close behind him. This time the two men did not hold back, but rode right up to MacDonald.

Grinning, MacDonald reached over and shook both men's hands. "I was wondering," he said, "if you two would ever dare get close enough for me to do that."

"The contagion is lifted," Canyon said. "Why not?"

"And you believe that, do you?"

"Sure."

"In that case, I have a request."

"What is it?" Canyon asked.

"We need guides if we're going to reach the Columbia. I haven't the foggiest notion of how to get there. Both our guide and scout died early on. Of course, we've been following a pretty detailed itinerary, but that doesn't mean much if you don't know the country. I was hoping that once we got free of the cholera, you two might consider guiding us at least as far as the Columbia.''

Canyon glanced at Sam, who grinned and shrugged, leaving it up to O'Grady.

"Okay, MacDonald," Canyon said. "Sam and I'll catch up to your wagon train before you leave the valley.''

The man brightened considerably. "I sure do appreciate it. Thanks.''

As Canyon and Sam spurred back up the slope, Wilder said, "Glad we're doin' this, hoss. I been itchin' to take another look at Oregon.''

As the two men rejoined the chiefs and started for the Nez Percé village, Canyon took one last look back at the knoll. These past two weeks in this encampment had not been at all unpleasant, he realized.

Some distance from the village, Canyon found a spot where he hoped he might be able to think undisturbed; he slumped to the ground, a tree at his back.

When he had told Kersten of his decision to guide the wagon train on to the Columbia, something he caught in her eyes told him she was reading more into this decision than was warranted. She too was going to join the wagon train and at once she had concluded that this was his reason for agreeing to guide the settlers the rest of the way to Oregon. But she had nothing to do with his decision. Canyon had already made sure Judge Fowler G. Langley had survived the cholera and was still with the wagons. But he could not tell her this. Even Sam did not know why Canyon was after Langley. Or what would have to be done when the two met finally.

O'Grady puffed on his pipe and stared into the gathering dusk. He guessed it didn't really matter what Kersten thought. He would let her think whatever it pleased her to think. The rest would be up to him. He had a job to do, and he had to do it.

But he could not take Kersten lightly. During that punishing flight from the Blackfoot, he had not treated her gently and she had fought him tooth and nail. But that was behind them, and during that ordeal a bond had been forged that could not easily be broken. Returning to the village this morning and seeing her, he had been startled at how swiftly she had recovered. With her standing close beside him in her doeskin dress, there had been no doubt that she was impossibly beautiful—and desirable.

"Oh, here you are."

Canyon was startled. He had not heard Kersten approaching. He got to his feet.

"Just taking a smoke," he told her.

"And thinking deeply—but with such a frown!"

"That so?"

"I hope you aren't having second thoughts."

"About guiding the wagon train?"

"Yes," she replied.

"I gave my word to MacDonald."

"I'm glad. I'll feel a lot safer with you and Sam guiding us."

"It's Sam who knows the country. Not me. He's been to Oregon before. I haven't."

"I don't care. I'm just glad you're going, too."

He looked at her and smiled. Her beauty was

breathtaking. "Looks like I'll be meeting your brother in a few weeks."

She kissed him then, hard on the lips. The sudden, unexpected shock of her passion startled him. He responded and found fire in her passion—and pulled her closer.

7

The wagon train had almost left the valley when Canyon, Sam, and Kersten overtook it. Trailing behind them were three heavily laden packhorses containing their gear. Canyon was willing to concede that the cholera had been licked; nevertheless, he did not intend to sleep in or near the wagons, nor join the settlers in any meals.

He and Sam would guide them through to the Columbia River and fill their pots with fresh game, a task Canyon would share gladly with the mountain man. But not with MacDonald or any of the other settlers. For since neither Canyon nor anyone else knew for sure what it was that had extinguished the contagion, there was no sense in Canyon or Sam— or Kersten—taking any chances. The cholera might flare up again among the settlers at any time. Canyon insisted on this, and MacDonald made no attempt to change his mind, understanding perfectly the need for caution.

The first full day of travel after Canyon and the others overtook the wagon train, the wagons lifted into the high pass leading from the valley, moving across chilly snow fields that had not yet completely melted. At this altitude the wind remained brisk, the sky clear, the thin air bracing. Some of the settlers trudging along beside the wagons had to keep a brisk pace to keep up, and all of them were laboring under the effort.

Canyon let his pony slow so that the wagons passed him by. When he found himself riding alongside the wagon containing Judge Fowler G. Langley's party, he increased the pony's gait and kept abreast of it. The judge was holding the ribbons guiding his four-horse team, and beside him on the seat sat a smaller, wiry man with narrow, suspicious eyes: Jake Gettis.

Glancing up at the judge, Canyon nodded to him. The judge nodded back. Langley seemed surprisingly fit for a man his age. He had a graying, well-cropped beard, sharp blue eyes, and a wide, expressive mouth. He did not look at all like a man still determined to assassinate a president. But then, Canyon mused, which man's countenance carries the truth hidden in his heart?

"You'd be Canyon O'Grady," Langley said, "the one who made us all clean up."

"I am."

"You think that's what killed the cholera?"

Canyon shrugged.

"Even if it didn't," Langley acknowledged, "we all smell a hell of a lot better."

"I noticed."

Gettis eyed Canyon suspiciously. "What're you doin' out here in these parts, O'Grady? You sound like you're from the East."

"That's the way all of you sound," Canyon reminded him casually.

"You ain't answered my question."

"Leave it be, Jake," said Langley.

Gettis shifted his eyes from Canyon and looked straight ahead. But it was clear to Canyon that inside his heart Jake Gettis was not letting it be. The man was suspicious by nature and it hadn't taken him long to question Canyon's presence. Canyon felt a grudging admiration for the man. As a bodyguard for Langley, he was acting precisely as he should.

And if Judge Langley was carrying the amount of gold it was rumored he was taking with him, neither he nor Gettis could afford to trust anyone in the wagon train, and certainly not any stranger who showed up at a Nez Percé encampment in eastern attire and equipment, then joined up with the train as it continued on to Oregon.

"I hear tell you're keeping away from the wagons still," Langley said to Canyon. "Still afraid of the cholera, are you?"

"It might return. How do we know it won't?"

"If that's so," asked Gettis, his eyes cold, "what're you doin' ridin' this close to our wagon right now?"

Canyon shrugged. "Could be I'm getting a mite careless."

Gettis eyed him shrewdly, obviously not buying Canyon's explanation. Again he looked away, leaving a chill in the air that was almost palpable.

Canyon decided it was about time for him to spur ahead, but he still had a few questions left. "I hope you did not lose any kin to the cholera," he said to Langley.

"Friends we lost. But no kin."

"Then you two are traveling alone?"

"What's that to you, O'Grady?" Gettis snapped.

"It helps me in figuring how to distribute manpower in case we get into trouble later. If you've got no children or women in the wagons, you can leave your wagon to help out.''

"You think we might be tangling with hostiles?'' Langley asked.

"Yes.''

"But those Indians back there in the valley were not hostile.''

"They were Nez Percé. It's the Blackfoot I'm thinking of.''

"We're ready to help any way we can, O'Grady,'' Langley assured Canyon. He glanced at his dour companion. "Isn't that so, Jake?''

"Sure. I guess.''

Langley smiled at O'Grady. "Jake means he'll be eager to help.''

"He'd better be,'' said Canyon. "It's his scalp, after all.'' With a quick wave, he peeled away from the wagon and then lifted his pony to a canter and rode to the head of the train. As he rode, he imagined he could feel the chill gaze of Jake Gettis resting on his back.

Jake frowned intently as he watched Canyon ride to the head of the wagons. "I don't trust that one, Judge,'' he said. "He ain't what he seems.''

"Now, Jake, who of us are what we seem?''

"That ain't the point. I think Canyon O'Grady's been sent after us.''

"By whom?''

"By Philbrick.''

"If so, it was a providential move. O'Grady might well have saved us from cholera.''

"I tell you I can smell trouble. It's in his eyes. He measured us both and found what he was after."

"I suppose it's possible, at that."

"Anything's possible where Philbrick is concerned. The man never gives up."

"He reminds me of you, Jake."

"I'll take that as a compliment, Judge. But you know what I feel about Philbrick and the rest of his jackals."

Langley chuckled. "Indeed I do, Jake. So what are you going to do?"

"Ain't much we can do now, Judge. This O'Grady is indispensable, it seems, to the safety and well-being of this wagon train. We've already made our bid to take over its direction and got nowhere."

"Our few followers succumbed to the cholera. It was a disaster I could not have foreseen, Jake."

"So that leaves us with O'Grady and the mountain man to see us through to Oregon," Gettis said. "I'll have to let O'Grady be until then. Meanwhile, I think I'll stay close to him. If he rides out alone tomorrow like his buddy did today, it would be a good idea for me to ride out also, keep an eye on him."

"My God! What for, Jake?"

"In case he has confederates coming to meet us from Oregon."

"That's highly unlikely, isn't it, Jake?"

"I never like to take chances, Judge."

"You never do, Jake—and for that I owe you."

"I'll have to borrow a saddle horse from the Mellons."

"You think they'll let you do that?" Langley asked.

Jake glanced at the judge, a slight smile on his

narrow face. "Well, maybe I'll have to pay them some."

Langley sighed. "Jake, your hand is always in the till."

"Maybe you'd rather I steal the horse."

Langley chuckled. "Help yourself, Jake. Help yourself. You have the key to the trunk."

Jake Gettis nodded and turned his attention to the trail ahead. It would be good to get his ass off this hard seat at that. He was already looking forward to tracking O'Grady tomorrow while the man scouted ahead of the wagons. This evening he would take out his pappy's Kentucky rifle and see to its priming.

Just in case.

Even as Jake Gettis considered the necessity of seeing to his rifle's priming, Sam Wilder rode into the wagon train, a young elk draped over the neck of his horse. He was greeted by pleased and excited settlers, who promptly divided the carcass and built great roaring fires to roast the meat.

Using the light of the cold stars arching over their encampment that evening, Kersten left her wagon and made her way through the darkness to Canyon's blanket. Afterward, he could tell she felt she had done him a good turn and expected him to be properly grateful. He didn't exactly see it that way, since he could tell from her response that he had done her just as good a turn. But he went along with her conceit and acted properly grateful.

They lay for a while side by side, content, and Canyon was close to dropping off when, without warning, Kersten turned her face to his and asked about Fern Song. From her tone it was clear she felt he owed her an explanation. At the village she had not mentioned the Indian woman. Only now, it seemed, did she feel safe asking about the Nez Percé woman.

"There's nothing to tell about Fern Song," he told her.

"Oh?"

"The way Sam tells it, Indian women don't put all that store by sleeping with a man, at least not the way white women do."

"I don't think I know what you mean," she replied, a hint of ice in her voice.

"I mean it's not so all-fired important to them, that's all."

"If that's so, why do you suppose she joined you out there?"

"She was just being hospitable. Besides, it was the chief who sent her."

"To comfort you."

"Yes. And to warm my couch at night." He grinned at her. "It got pretty damn chilly up on that knoll."

He saw her stiffen slightly. "And you just let her do it?"

"Of course."

"I see."

He didn't like her tone or the direction this interrogation was taking, and he was about to turn away from her. Sensing his reaction, she softened immediately, and purring like a great cat, she reached over and proceeded to arouse him once more.

They made love a second time and he enjoyed it and did not mind showing it. But through it all, he could sense a part of her watching him coldly, holding a part of herself back. When she left his blanket to return to her own sleeping bag, he watched her vanish into the darkness and found himself thinking, not of her, but of Fern Song.

The Indian woman had been so much more honest.

Close to midday, Canyon found a likely spot for his noon camp, a shaded spot with an ice-cold spring oozing from a cleft in a rock. He dismounted alongside it, rested his back against a boulder, and feasted on the pemmican Fern Song had pressed on him when he rode out of the Nez Percé village. He was washing the meal down with the icy spring water when a lone Indian appeared on the skyline to his right. The Indian made no effort to keep out of sight and simply sat astride his pony. Motionless. Waiting. Even though a half-mile or so separated them, Canyon knew it was a Blackfoot warrior.

Something about the Indian was vaguely familiar.

A strange sense of the inevitability of what must follow came over Canyon. Or was it resignation? He only knew that the Blackfoot was waiting for him—and that he was destined to ride out and meet this warrior. He rested awhile longer, refilled his canteen, then mounted up.

The closer he got to the Blackfoot, the more certain he became that—as he had surmised dimly from the first—this was the same warrior whose life he had spared a few weeks before. And then he was certain of it. He almost laughed aloud. Who was it who said only the good Lord could spare a man from the consequences of his good deeds?

Ahead of Canyon, Eagle Feather wheeled his

mount and vanished beyond a ridge. The agent understood perfectly. The warrior had already selected a place for this final combat, and he was to follow him to it.

Canyon crested the ridge and checked his Henry's load as he spurred after the Blackfoot. Soon he was crossing a gully half-filled with snow, the tracks of the Blackfoot's pony clearly visible. Lifting out of it, he found himself riding onto a high plateau, a harsh landscape pocked with brush, rocks, and boulders. Some of the boulders were as large as houses, patches of snow still crouching in their shadows. At this height, a knifing wind cut cruelly at him. He kept on, his narrowed eyes on the Blackfoot's tracks.

Occasionally, he caught sight of the Blackfoot—but only for a moment, as the Indian kept far enough ahead of him to remain out of sight.

Eagle Feather allowed himself a ghost of a smile. Now at last there would be an end to his quest. The arrogance of this white man in letting him live had shriveled his spirit. Such a gift from such a source had contaminated him. He was unclean. Only with this white-eyes dead could Eagle Feather ever again live in peace.

The night before the settlers had moved their wagons out, Eagle Feather had had a powerful dream. In it, he had seen a lone wolf bring down a great bull buffalo by attacking him head-on. The lobo wolf attacked repeatedly, giving the great beast no quarter until at last the buffalo's spirit had been broken. Sensing his opportunity, the wolf went for the buffalo's flanks, hamstringing him, and when the great beast crashed to the dust, the wolf went for his throat.

Now, watching Big Shoulders ride after him, the dream-vision of that bull buffalo's violent death throes were still clear in Eagle Feather's memory. Just as the wolf had buried its fangs in the buffalo's throat, Eagle Feather would close his fingers about Big Shoulder's windpipe, throttling his spirit and preventing it from following him into the other world, leaving it to wander in torment on this desolate plain, forever severed from its body.

Even if this dream were a false vision sent by evil spirits bent on destroying Eagle Feather, it did not matter. His foe was before him now, riding swiftly after him. Their upcoming battle could not be avoided. But Eagle Feather did not think the dream-vision was a lie. He was supremely confident in its ability to guide his actions. Was it not a fact that Big Shoulders had spared him when he could have taken Eagle Feather's life? A man who could do such a thing had no steel in his heart. He was a contemptible weakling, a white-eyes, after all.

He did not have a warrior's heart.

At last, Canyon reached a kind of natural amphitheater, a flat patch of frozen ground enclosed by a semicircle of massive boulders. On the hard ground, there was only a ghostly trace of Eagle Feather's pony's tracks. He had been here and was gone. Canyon was getting impatient. When would this fool Blackfoot come to earth, so they could finish this matter?

As if in answer to his silent query, he heard the sudden clatter of unshod hooves and turned to face the Blackfoot's charge. He was coming at Canyon from behind a boulder without a battle cry, his painted warrior's face grim with resolve, his lance lowered. Canyon wheeled his mount and brought up the Henry. He fired in haste and missed, and was forced to parry the lance with the rifle barrel, but the tip of the Indian's lance caught him high on his shoulder.

It did not penetrate, but its force was enough to topple Canyon off his horse. He lost control of the Henry and came down hard on his back. Shaken by the fall, he was scrambling after the rifle when the Blackfoot charged again, swinging down at him with his war club. He caught Canyon a glancing blow on the side of his head, then wheeled and charged again. Canyon reached back for his holstered Colt. As he brought it up to fire, the Blackfoot clubbed the weapon from his grasp.

Again Canyon went for his Henry, but he only had time to grab the barrel and swing its stock at the onrushing warrior. The Blackfoot's heavy stone club glanced off the rifle stock, coming down on Canyon's shoulder instead. The blow sent a numbing shudder down his entire right side. But it was not the fatal, debilitating blow to the skull it could have been, and ignoring its effects, Canyon reached up and managed to grab the Indian's thigh as he charged past. His powerful fingers digging into the bronzed flesh, he tore the Blackfoot from his mount.

There was no thought in Canyon's mind now, no cold deliberation—only a surcharged fury that would brook no containment. He flung himself on his enemy, his hunting knife in his hand. Lifting its long blade aloft, he tried to plunge it into the Blackfoot's heart. But as he struggled to do so, he became coldly aware that he was battling a man filled with an insensate fury that imparted to him an almost superhuman strength.

But Canyon's desire to live gave him a strength just as powerful. Dropping the knife in favor of his sledging fists, he began to batter the Indian about the head and shoulders with such a wild, mindless fury that the warrior lost the ability to fight back or protect himself. After one particularly vicious blow to the Indian's temple, Canyon saw the Indian's eyes roll back in his head. O'Grady promptly hauled Eagle Feather to his feet and kicked him savagely in the groin, then flung him back against the face of a boulder with an explosive, savage force. The back of the Blackfoot's head slammed against the boulder with numbing force, and the man crumpled to the ground.

At that moment, swaying over his downed opponent, Canyon realized that if he could manage it, he would like to rend this maddened savage limb from limb. Gasping for air, he decided to break off the battle for a second or two to get his breath. He backed up. The Blackfoot stirred and looked coldly up at him. Canyon glanced about him for his revolver, assuming the Indian was injured too badly from the blow to his head to come at him immediately.

He was wrong.

Eagle Feather leapt to his feet and charged Canyon, a long skinning knife in his right hand. There was nothing fancy about the attack, no dodging or feinting. It was a simple, straightforward head-on charge that under the circumstances made no sense at all. Canyon ducked to one side. As the Blackfoot charged past him, the point of his knife slashed through O'Grady's jacket, its tip catching in the heavy buckskin fabric, ripping the weapon from the Indian's grasp.

Snatching up the Blackfoot's dropped lance, Canyon spun about to face his next charge. Though he had only his stone war club left, Eagle Feather did not hesitate, and in a move so foolhardy Canyon could not fully comprehend it, the Blackfoot once more flung himself straight at him.

Canyon dug in his heels and kept the lance steady. Only at the last moment did the charging Indian attempt to parry the lance with his war club. But Canyon simply shifted his feet slightly and thrust the lance suddenly forward, slashing through his adversary's right forearm, its long steel blade sinking into his shoulder. Canyon heard as well as felt the Blackfoot's startled gasp, as if this were something that should not have happened.

Eagle Feather sagged to the ground. Canyon stepped quickly forward and, placing one foot on the Indian's shoulder, yanked the lance free, a crimson freshet of blood pulsing from the slashing wound. Panting slightly, Canyon stepped back and gazed down at the Blackfoot. The warrior looked up at Canyon, his face frozen into a mask of bitter contempt.

"Finish it, White-eyes," he cried.

"I am waiting," Canyon told him grimly. "Give me time."

"Once again the white-eyes cannot kill. He is a woman."

Canyon realized he had no choice. This Indian

courted death—his or Canyon's—with a ferocity and a constancy that would brook no denial this side of hell.

He flung aside the lance and kicked the Indian senseless with one well-aimed blow from the tip of his riding boot. Then he grabbed hold of the warrior's wrist, flung the bloody form over the neck of his appaloosa, and rode back the way he had come until he reached a drop-off he had noticed earlier. He dismounted and peered down into the ravine at the tangle of boulders far below. Satisfied the drop was sufficient to kill the Indian outright, Canyon returned to his pony, pulled the Indian off its neck, and dragged him to the edge of the precipice.

Before he could fling the body over, however, the Blackfoot twisted to sudden, violent life. On his feet less than a foot from him, Eagle Feather's smile was terrible to see as he reached out with both hands and closed his iron fingers around Canyon's throat. Gasping, Canyon tried to peel the fingers away. But it was no use as the Indian bore him to the ground under him, the steady gout of his blood pouring past Canyon's face as his fingers tightened like steel cables about the agent's windpipe. O'Grady struggled desperately, but a gray darkness soon blotted out the savage's face. A roaring sounded in Canyon's ears and he felt himself falling . . .

Then, as in a dream, a distant shot sounded.

The steel fingers about Canyon's throat loosened. His breath rushed into his lungs. The weight on his chest was miraculously gone. Coughing raggedly, he rolled away from the body sprawled beside him, sat up, and opened his eyes.

What he saw astounded him.

The Blackfoot warrior was dead beside him, a hole in the back of his skull where a round had entered it not a moment before. Standing up, Canyon looked quickly, eagerly about him for his benefactor. But he saw no one.

Could it have been Sam?

But what would Sam be doing out here? And that bullet had not come from a Hawken. Otherwise the Blackfoot's entire face would have been blown away. It was painful for him to swallow, let alone raise his voice. So he did not cry out or try to hail whoever it was who had saved him. Instead, he dragged the dead Blackfoot's sprawled body closer to the edge of the drop and booted him over.

Then he pulled the appaloosa toward him and mounted up. First he would retrieve his Henry and his revolver. Then he would find a stream and wash off the Indian's blood from his face and clothes as well as he could. After that, he would seek out fresh venison to bring down for the settlers.

It would be a pleasure to kill for a good reason.

It was dark when Jake Gettis slipped silently into the judge's wagon and placed his long Kentucky rifle back in its case, but not before he had lit a lamp and cleaned it thoroughly.

He and the judge were sitting around their fire now, the sounds of the camp all around them. Judge Langley had reheated portions of the food he had cooked for supper earlier and Jake ate silently, the way a man does when he is very hungry and has a lot to think over. After he finished the venison and beans, swilled down with scalding coffee, the judge told him to relax, that he would clean the plates and the frying pan. Jake took out his pipe and lit up, watching the judge scour his tin plate with a fistful of sand.

"You want to tell me why you cleaned your rifle just now?" Judge Langley asked, rinsing the plate in a bucket of water.

"I used it today."

"Not on O'Grady, surely. He rode in hours ago with a buck he brought down. You just finished a portion of it."

"No. Not on O'Grady."

"You fired at some game?"

"At a Blackfoot. At least I think it was one of them. I can never tell one Indian from another."

"My God, Jake. You want to start an Indian uprising?"

"It was only one Indian."

"You going to stop beating around the bush and tell me what happened?"

"I'm trying to figure it out myself, Judge. It was queer."

"Talk straight or I'll bend this frying pan over your head."

"The thing is, if O'Grady is after us, I did a dumb thing. I saved that Irishman's life."

"You what?"

"You heard me. I saved his life. But it's hard to describe. I swear, it looked to me like O'Grady and this Blackfoot were having a duel."

"A duel? Out here?"

"I know it sounds crazy. But that's how it looked like to me."

Exasperated, the judge said, "Jake, will you please start from the beginning."

Jake puffed a moment on his pipe, then spoke. "I followed O'Grady for most of the morning. He was making a noon camp when this Indian appeared on the horizon. Like I said, it was queer. He just sat his pony on the ridge and waited. O'Grady saw him, mounted up, and rode toward him. The Indian turned and led O'Grady a short distance until he came to a plateau. Then he came at O'Grady with a lance, burst at him from behind a boulder, straight on—no preliminaries. When the two were unhorsed, they battled hand to hand, and when it looked as if O'Grady was going to be throttled, I raised my rifle and . . . took matters into my own hand."

"You mean you shot the Indian."

"Yes. It was quite a distance and I might have missed and killed O'Grady instead." Jake smiled grimly at the judge. "Maybe I was just testing the rifle after all this time. I wanted to see if it could go fetch 'em, like it did for my pappy at New Orleans."

"And did it?"

"It only took one shot. The Indian toppled forward and O'Grady kicked him into a ravine and rode off. You said you saw him ride in with a dead buck. He went after that buck as if that were the only reason for him being out there. His battle with that Blackfoot seemed to have no effect on him."

"And it was a duel, you say?"

"I am sure of it. I think maybe he knew the Indian from somewhere, had a grudge to settle, maybe—so they met out there to settle matters."

"And you played God and stepped in."

"Like I said before, it's up to MacDonald and O'Grady—and that mountain man—to help us get to Oregon. He's more valuable to us alive than dead."

The judge smiled. "And you saw no sign of Philbrick's confederates coming to meet him."

Jake chuckled. "Nary a one."

"If O'Grady knew that Indian, maybe he's not an easterner, after all. Him and that mountain man are thick as fleas, don't forget. And Sam looks like he's been out here as long as these mountains. And as sure as God made yellow buttercups, Philbrick did not send *him*."

"Yeah, Judge. I thought of that, too."

"So maybe we can relax. And since you saved this O'Grady's life, you are responsible for his safety from now on. You're his guardian angel."

"Maybe so," Jake said gloomily, drawing on his pipe, "and maybe Philbrick didn't send him—but I still don't trust that Irishman."

The judge chuckled and filled his own pipe.

8

The pass beckoned in the distance, a welcome break in the solid ranks of snow-capped peaks shouldering into the bright afternoon sky. A ridge on its southern flank was covered with a thick stand of pine and reminded Canyon of a Mohawk's scalp lock. So sheer were the walls of the pass, it looked as if they had been sliced out of the mountain by the strokes of some monstrous ax.

Sam had already scouted the pass and there was more-than-enough fresh meat for the settlers, so he had joined Canyon and Kersten when he saw them riding ahead of the wagon train.

"That pass is such a pretty sight," Kersten remarked. "I wonder the poets have not come out here to put it in verse."

"Give them time, Kersten," Canyon remarked. "Give them time."

Sam chuckled. "You don't think that's such a good idea?"

Canyon shook his head. "I don't see how the words of any poet could capture that sight, or should even try."

Kersten laughed. "Maybe you're right at that."

Canyon glanced back. The evenly spaced wagons

were strung out in a perfect line as they crossed the gently sloping parkland, resembling a fleet of schooners plowing through a sea of grass. As his eyes swept to the right, he caught sight of an antelope herd moving off in long, soaring leaps. It was indeed a truly beautiful country, Canyon realized. He didn't think it was possible for even an Irish poet to do justice to it.

"What's that?" Sam muttered. "A bear?"

Canyon followed his gaze and saw what appeared to be a bear in the tall grass a quarter-mile ahead of them. The animal was making directly for them and was doing its best to maintain an upright position.

Reaching for his Henry, Canyon cranked in a fresh round, then rested the rifle across his pommel.

"The way it's comin' at us, hoss," said Sam, "I'm thinkin' it's a rogue."

"Are you going to shoot it?" Kersten asked, alarmed.

"He might have to," Sam told her. "Rogues are a little crazy. I've heard tell of rogues who've attacked teams of horses."

"Wait a minute," said Canyon, peering with narrowed eyes at the oncoming bear. "That's no bear."

"No, by grannies," Sam cried, "it ain't!"

"It's Tim Flannery," Canyon said.

Both men spurred ahead of Kersten, heading directly for the struggling figure. They dismounted on the run when they reached him and found Flannery to be in such grim shape that he was struggling just to keep upright. At sight of them, he gave up trying and collapsed to the ground, mumbling crazily, his words barely coherent. His buckskin shirt was in tatters, his legs blistered from ugly burns. He had been beaten with methodical cruelty about the head and shoulders and his hands were scabbed, bloody claws. Each finger had lost its fingernail. He was not a pleasant sight.

Riding up behind them, Canyon heard Kersten's gasp as she gazed down at Flannery.

Wilder knelt in the grass and bent over his old companion. "Tim, it's me. Sam."

"Blackfoot," Flannery gasped, his clawed hand wavering at the pass behind him. "They's waitin' in the pass. Ambush!"

Sam took the nearly ruined scarecrow of a man in his arms and stood up. Heading for his mount, he looked quickly around and spotted a ridge a half-mile south. Turning to Canyon, he pointed to it.

"Canyon, help me get Flannery up on my horse, then go back and tell MacDonald to get the wagons to that ridge—and not to worry about stayin' in line. I'm headin' there right now." Sam looked at Kersten. "Kersten, you'll be comin' with me. Flannery needs nursin'."

Her face pale, Kersten simply nodded.

Canyon lifted Flannery up onto the pommel of Sam's horse, then stepped back as the mountain man turned his mount and headed for the ridge, Kersten keeping pace with him.

Canyon mounted up then and rode back to the wagons at a hard gallop.

Canyon saw the Blackfoot war party pouring out through the pass. Aware that any chance of an ambush had been lost, they were trying to cut off the wagons before they reached the ridge.

At once Canyon left the wagons strung out behind

him and rode straight for the hard-charging Indians, intent on blunting their attack or at least scattering their war party. When he found himself within rifle range of the nearest Blackfoot, he wound his reins around the saddle horn, lifted his Henry to his shoulder, and opened fire. Cranking swiftly, he sent a storm of hot lead into their midst that not only cut down the lead Indian, but spread consternation and panic through the ranks of the war party. As Canyon swept on toward them, his merciless fire continuing unabated, they turned in disarray and scattered.

Seeing this, Canyon whipped his pony around and headed for the ridge. The lead wagons were already climbing a steep trail leading up onto it, and in some cases it looked as if the grade would be too steep for the horses. But with whips crackling over their plunging bodies, they managed to keep going. First one, then another wagon gained the ridge. One of the last wagons rocked dangerously and it appeared for a moment that it might slip back, but the driver, on his feet and cursing a blue streak, kept the horses going. It cleared the slope and gained the ridge, and soon after, all seven wagons had pulled up close into a stand of aspen.

When Canyon himself reached the ridge, he dismounted and, with a smart slap to the appaloosa's rump, sent it toward the wagons. Then he returned with his Henry to the rocks lining the crest of the ridge and slipping down behind one, got ready for the Indians' inevitable assault. It was not long before men were pouring down into the rocks to join him. When Sam reached him, Canyon asked about Tim Flannery.

"Kersten's takin' care of him back in one of the

wagons. She's gettin' help from some other women. Looks like we're a part of this wagon train now, whether we like it or not." Sam gazed out at the Blackfoot war party. They had regrouped after Canyon turned for the ridge and were showing off their horsemanship as they raced back and forth in front of the ridge, brandishing their lances and filling the air with their battle cries. "Them bastards," Sam muttered. "It's a wonder to me how old Tim got loose to warn us."

"The important thing is he did," said Canyon. Looking about him, he saw MacDonald clustered with three men, and farther down Jake Gettis and Judge Fowler Langley. Gettis was holding a long Kentucky rifle while the judge had a fancy, single-shot hunting rifle that looked as if it had been specially made for him—but not for this kind of hunting.

Abe Mellon dropped down beside Sam.

"I count twenty redskins," he told Sam.

Sam nodded. "My estimate, too."

Abe Mellon was a husky, broad-shouldered young man with a black beard cut close to his chin, and eyes so dark they looked like they were made from anthracite. His rifle looked well-cared-for. When Canyon had ridden back to turn the wagons, he had learned that Abe had a pregnant wife in his wagon and was desperate to protect her from these raging Indians.

On the other side of Sam were Phil Turner and Bill Walsh. All that Walsh had to fight with was a huge Walker Colt, but it would have to do—and undoubtedly would come in handy in close combat.

Phil Turner held a battered, nondescript rifle and had stuck a revolver in his belt.

"Here they come," Sam said softly.

Canyon looked back at the Indians. Showtime was over, it seemed. They had stopped galloping back and forth in front of the ridge and were now riding straight for it.

"Hold your fire," Canyon called out to the men. "Make each shot count!"

But the Blackfoot had just as good sense. At a signal from their war chief—a warrior sporting a single red feather—they dropped from their ponies and vanished into the tall grass. Not a one would reappear until they were at the foot of the ridge, Canyon realized, making a break for the rocks at the foot of the slope that would give them additional cover as they charged up to the ridge.

"This ain't goin' to be pretty," Sam muttered, as they all waited for the Indians to reappear.

Canyon could only nod.

A glance around at the others told him that the men were just as edgy as Sam—and for good reason. Once these Blackfoot started up the slope, it would mean hand-to-hand combat.

"I sure hope it gets dark soon," Bill Walsh whispered nervously.

"Why's that?" Sam asked.

"Indians never attack at night."

Sam's laugh was short, bitter. "In that case, Bill, as soon as it gets dark, you go right to sleep. We'll wake you, come mornin'. If any of us are still wearin' our scalps."

"You mean it ain't true?"

"Where'd you hear such a fool thing?"

"I read it somewhere," Walsh admitted ruefully. "I suppose it's a pretty silly idea at that."

"It sure as hell is," Sam snapped. "The redskin does most of his fighting by the light of the moon when there is one—and in pitch dark when it ain't up there to light his way."

Phil Turner, pretty anxious by this time, craned his neck in an effort to catch sight of a Blackfoot moving toward them through the grass. He didn't have any luck. And neither did Canyon or any of the others. But the Blackfoot were down there, moving swiftly toward them.

"I can't see a single one of 'em," complained Turner. Before anyone could stop him, he stood up to get a better view of the thick grassland below. A shot from a clump of grass less than twenty yards from the base of the ridge sent a slug ricocheting off a rock inches from his head. Turner ducked down as quickly as if the shot had found its mark.

"Maybe you can't see 'em," Sam drawled, chuckling, "but they sure as hell can see you. The next time you stick your head up like that, you'll get it turned inside out. That redskin's got your range now."

Turner could only swallow and nod. He was a pale, very shaken young man.

"That's right," seconded Canyon. "Keep your head down, Turner. We're going to need all the firepower we can muster."

Turner shrank still lower in the rocks, his face chalk-white.

"I think it's time we spread out," Canyon told Sam. "What do you think?"

"Good idea. And warn each man to keep down. These Blackfoot are damn good marksmen."

Canyon moved out.

The first attack came at dusk. It was a foolish move by a brave eager to count coup and make a name for himself. He rose out of the grass, firing as he came, and dashed toward the ridge, picking his way through the rocks and darting up the slope straight for Canyon. He was better than halfway up before Canyon was able to plant a slug in his bare chest.

But the warrior kept on coming.

Canyon stood up to get a better shot. But fire from other Blackfoot charging after the first one filled the air with singing lead and he was forced to duck low. The brave was almost on him when Canyon swung up his Henry and got off another shot. The round singed the Indian's flesh in his side just under his rib cage, which was as good as a miss. With no time to crank another round into the Henry, Canyon was reaching for his knife when MacDonald blew the Blackfoot's head apart.

Levering swiftly, Canyon opened up then on another Indian halfway up the slope, cutting him down. The rocks just below the ridge were swarming now with Blackfoot, and from all quarters came the rattle of rifle fire and the occasional boom of Bill Walsh's Walker Colt. The firing lasted for no more than a few minutes, however. As quickly as it began, the attack ended and the Indians fled back down the slope to vanish once more into the deep grass.

Canyon glanced over at MacDonald. The young wagon master waved to him, grinning. Canyon waved back as Sam ducked down beside him.

"How many of the hostiles did we bag?" Canyon asked.

"I counted at least five dead, but they's plenty more where them came from. That Gettis feller has a mighty long reach with that Kentucky rifle of his. I saw him stop one at least three hundred yards back the moment the man showed his painted face above the grass."

"Did we lose any?"

"Not a one. And Phil Turner accounted for one of them. He's a real cool customer when the chips are down. Waited until the redskin was on top of him before he blasted the son of a bitch. Said he wanted to make sure."

"I heard Bill Walsh's cannon."

"Yep. It sure was thunderin'. He knocked one Blackfoot ass over teakettle. But he's still shaking."

A fleeting grin passed over Canyon's face. "Let him shake, as long as he doesn't run."

"All we got to worry about now is the next attack," Sam said. "And it'll come in the dark, no matter what Phil Turner read. If they press us too hard, we might have to pull back to the wagons."

"I don't want to think about that."

"Neither do I," Sam said gloomily.

When darkness came, the moon sailed into the heavens, gleaming like a newly minted silver dollar. If the defenders on the ridge were grateful for the light, the Blackfoot had to be just as pleased. Now they could see what they were doing.

With sudden, chilling war cries, the Blackfoot rose out of the grass and charged the ridge. Two Blackfoot led the assault on Canyon's position. He stopped one with a slug in his gullet, then caught the second one high in the chest, slamming him back down among the rocks. It was apparent by now that Canyon's rapid-firing Henry had attracted the attention of the Blackfoot war party.

The Indians had probably already heard some word of the Henry's potential and were anxious to take the repeating rifle from him. More than a trophy, it could be a weapon that distinguished its owner and assured him victory in any encounter with his single-shot adversaries. However, wanting Canyon's rifle was one thing, taking it from him was something else again. Again and again, the Henry's devastating fire took a cruel toll of the attacking Blackfoot. Sooner than before, they cut off their attack and melted back into the night.

Not until midnight did the Blackfoot make another assault. This one did not come in a howling, head-on attack. The first Canyon knew of it was when he heard the heel of a moccasin strike the surface of a rock behind him. Swinging his Colt around, he fired up at the figure hurtling at him out of the night. The body struck Canyon a numbing blow, but he managed to fling the brave off him, and when he looked down at him, he saw the hole in his chest left there by his Colt. The warrior was already a dead man when he struck him.

All around Canyon now came the grunts and cries of hand-to-hand combat. Another brave leapt out of the night at him. This time there was no time for Canyon to fire at his attacker. He unsheathed his knife and managed to duck under the warrior's hatchet. The Indian reached for Canyon's Henry, and this was his undoing. Canyon drove his knife deep into the brave's unprotected chest and heard a gasp. He withdrew the knife and felt the surge of hot blood rushing out after it, then he booted the dying warrior down the slope into the rocks below.

Sam was beside him. "Move back," Sam told him. "To the wagons!"

Canyon raised his voice to echo Sam's call and immediately the rest of the ridge's defenders left their positions and, firing as they went, raced back across the narrow flat. Ragged fire from the circle of wagons helped discourage some of the Blackfoot, but not all of them, and the battle raged in and around the wagons. Only a few of the attacking warriors made it inside the wagon's perimeter, and those few who did were disposed of by the defenders, usually with sidearms at close range.

Abe Mellon's pregnant wife, Jane, had waited calmly while one savage approached her in her wagon. He was undoing his breechclout when she shot him in the stomach with an old but well-primed dueling pistol Abe had given her.

One irate woman, her two children crouching behind her skirts, brained an Indian with an iron frying pan, and by the time she was done with him, his head was flatter than the pan.

The attackers were beaten off, finally, and after that the night grew quiet. Too quiet.

Near dawn, Kersten screamed, a cry that made the hair on the back of Canyon's head stand straight up. He was on his way to visit Tim Flannery, and it was from this wagon that the scream came. Two quick steps brought Canyon to it. He vaulted in through the back of the wagon and saw Kersten flat on her back beside Flannery, a naked Indian on top of her, a knife held over his head. Before the Blackfoot could plunge it into Kersten's breast, Canyon shattered the Indian's skull with the stock of his Henry. Then he dragged him off Kersten and flung him out of the wagon. In a minute the rest of the company had hauled him out of sight, as if they were disposing of a piece of garbage.

Enclosing Kersten in his arms, he let her cry herself out. It didn't take long. She was as furious with herself for letting the Indian get that close to her as she was at the Indian for doing so. When she had calmed down, Canyon took the opportunity to check on Flannery. The mountain man was unconscious.

"He's been that way," Kersten told Canyon, "ever since we reached this wagon."

"He's missing all the excitement," Canyon told her, trying to ease the tension.

"Yes."

"He'll be furious when he comes out of it."

"I wish I were missing it." She began to cry again.

One of the women climbed into the wagon and took her gently and helped her down from the wagon, uttering soft words of comfort to her as she did so. Canyon was pleased. At a time like this a woman needed the comfort of another woman.

Not a man.

Sam joined him in the wagon. "Kersten goin' to be all right?"

"I hope so. The Indian didn't get a chance to take her."

Sam nodded, then rested his gaze on Flannery. "How's Tim?"

"He's still out of it. Completely. He had no idea what was going on right beside him."

"There's someone else I'm worrying about."

"Who?"

"Samantha Riley. In the next wagon."

"I've heard about her. She the one lost her husband and kids to the cholera?"

"And before that, on her way to Fort Billings in a single wagon, she lost her mother and her sister to the Blackfoot."

"So I heard. She still acting queer?"

"This horrible business with the Indians hasn't helped any. I'm thinking she's about to do something crazy. Take a look at her, will you, Canyon?"

"Is there no one with her?"

"Just Kersten for a while there. The rest of the women are with their husbands, helping them keep their weapons ready."

"I'll go take a look at her. Next wagon, you said?"

"Yes. If you think she might go berserk, we might have to tie her down. But I wouldn't like to do that."

"What does MacDonald say?"

"He agrees with me. She might go off her nut."

"I'll take a look." Canyon jumped lightly down out of the wagon, Sam following. They caught sight of MacDonald passing close by and told him that Canyon was going to look in on Samantha Riley. The wagon master seemed relieved and hurried off, Sam with him.

Squaring his shoulders, Canyon stepped up into Samantha Riley's wagon. Her hands riveted to the rocking chair's arms, she rocked steadily. The wagon shook slightly from the steady motion, and he could hear her singing—very low and softly—a hymn. The constant rocking in her chair Canyon had been prepared for, and the singing of the hymn as well. But not at the look in the woman's eyes as she glanced up at him. They were wide and staring, as if they were witnessing a horror worse than any nightmare.

Canyon knew of Samantha, but this was the first time he had met her. She looked formidable. Her face was square, her mouth as wide as a man's, her forehead flat, her tightly curled gray hair had been flattened to her skull by a hair net. A dark, knit shawl was thrown over her shoulders and her muslin skirts barely covered the tops of her high-button black shoes.

"Hello, Samantha," Canyon said. "How are you getting on?"

Samantha closed her eyes, rested her head back, and continued to sing the hymn, the rocker moving at a slightly faster pace now.

Canyon took a deep breath and tried again. "We're all worried about you. You going to be all right alone here? Do you need anything?"

It was, Canyon knew, a stupid question. But he was at a complete loss as to how to proceed with this distraught woman rocking her way through the hours, trying somehow to cope with the loss of so many she had held dear.

Abruptly, Samantha moved her head and stared at him with a startling fierceness. "Take the knife," she hissed. "Cut out their black hearts."

"What's that, Samantha?"

"The butcher knife," she told him, grinning horribly. "Use it on them."

"Sure, Samantha," Canyon said, backing away. "I'll be sure to do that."

Sam was right, Canyon realized. This woman was no longer responsible for her actions. Grief had driven her mad. Even so, Canyon had no desire to tie the woman up. Somehow, that seemed excessive. Samantha Riley had suffered enough without that final indignity.

"You promise to stay right here, Samantha?"

Her mad grin faded.

"Do you?"

She nodded carefully, slyly, the rate of her rocking slowing some.

Canyon backed up quickly and dropped to the ground, eager to get away from Samantha and the terrible emptiness in her eyes.

As dawn broke, the wagons' defenders moved back to their positions in the rocks bordering the ridge. What they saw was heartening. Well out of range, a small cluster of braves had gathered in the grass around their chief, Red Feather. There seemed to be much arm-waving and lots of agitated palaver. It was a war council, no doubt of it. At the same time two braves were moving off through the grass, heading toward the Blackfoot's ponies grazing in the distance.

"I like that," Sam said to Canyon. "Them two braves aren't havin' any more of this nonsense. They're announcing to the rest of the war party that they no longer believe in this war chief's magic. They're washing their hands of this business. Too many losses is the reason, I figure."

Judge Langley and Jake Gettis approached.

"What do you make of this?" the judge asked Sam, indicating the Indians with a sharp glance.

"The way I see it, they're tryin' to decide what to do next. Continue to attack or go home."

"What do you think they'll do?" Gettis asked.

"Beats me," Sam replied. "But the fact is they were counting on an ambush in that pass. That would've meant a quick painless massacre with a minimum of casualties. This way they've run into a buzz saw, and they know it."

"Then they'll move out," Langley said.

"Didn't say that." Sam sent a dagger of tobacco juice at the ground. "They still got their pride. They've taken a few hits and want to get even. This is still a big wagon train with many scalps and plenty of loot, don't forget."

"In that case," said Gettis, patting his rifle, "maybe I could send something out there to convince that war chief to go home."

"You think you can reach that far?" Canyon asked.

"I'd have to be pretty lucky."

"Yes, you would," said Canyon. "But maybe it wouldn't hurt to try."

"No, it wouldn't," Gettis said, smiling grimly, his eyes narrowing as he estimated the distance.

"I'd say that's close to a thousand yards," Sam said.

"That's about what I'm figurin', too," said Gettis, raising his rifle with infinite deliberation. He had evidently walked over with it already loaded and primed.

Canyon could see Gettis testing the wind, then watched as he lifted the rifle slightly to compensate for the distance. Gettis went perfectly still for an instant, and when the detonation came, it was with the slightest possible nudge of the trigger. A second after the rifle's crack echoed off the rocks, one of the braves standing beside Red Feather dropped. His companions broke back in consternation.

"You missed Red Feather," chided the judge softly.

"Yeah," Gettis said, spitting a ball into the barrel and reaching for his ramrod. "So I did. But I got the distance now."

Kersten's scream riveted the four men. Canyon turned to see Samantha Riley rushing toward the crest of the ridge, Kersten in pursuit. There was a huge carving knife in Samantha's hand.

"Stop her!' " cried Kersten. "She's gone mad."

That's the way it looked, all right, as the older woman dodged past one man and then another who tried to catch her. With amazing agility, she swept down the slope, slipping through the rocks, screaming like a banshee, the huge butcher knife in her upraised fist gleaming wickedly in the early-morning sun. Her destination was clear enough: the Blackfoot war party.

Dropping his rifle, Canyon went after her, but by the time he reached the flat, Samantha was a good distance from him, covering the ground swiftly as she approached the Blackfoot. The Indians had seen her coming and could hear her screams, but they were holding their ground, obviously transfixed by the apparition bearing down on them. A few of the Blackfoot began yelling taunts at her. Others began joking, slapping their thighs.

Canyon overtook Samantha and, unwilling to brave

the butcher knife, tackled her from behind. She went down hard, the knife slipping from her grasp. Canyon swept up the knife, thrust it into his belt, then pulled Samantha up onto her feet.

Screaming, she struck him in the face with such force that he rocked back, more startled than hurt. The blow caught his attention, however, and with the Blackfoot now racing toward them, Canyon realized he had no time to reason with the woman. He clipped her solidly on the chin and caught her as she sank, unconscious, into his arms, flung her over his shoulder, then started at a run for the rocks below the ridge.

But Samantha was not a light burden and Canyon was soon staggering while he was still at least fifty yards from the ridge. Behind him, the Blackfoot's rifle fire erupted. Canyon increased his pace, aware of covering fire coming from the ridge. He heard the pounding feet of a Blackfoot warrior closing on him from behind. Abruptly, a heavy hand smashed down onto Canyon's shoulder, spinning him around and causing him to spill Samantha onto the ground.

He spun to face the Blackfoot, drawing Samantha's butcher knife as he did so. The warrior was less than a foot from him and was raising his hatchet over his head. Canyon did not wait. He sprang on the warrior and thrust the knife deep into his side. The Indian dropped his hatchet, staggering back, and went down on one knee, a look of pure astonishment on his face.

Turning away from him, Canyon reached down for Samantha. A distant rifle shot sounded from the ridge. Glancing back, Canyon saw Red Feather stop suddenly, a hole in his chest. He dropped the knife he was holding and crumpled to the grass. Behind the war chief the rest of the Blackfoot, enraged by their leader's fall, continued to race toward Canyon. He flung Samantha over his shoulder once more and continued on to the ridge. By keeping after Canyon, however, the warriors brought themselves within range of the settlers' rifles. As the withering fire opened up on them, they began to melt away like wax in the noonday sun.

Canyon reached the rocks and started up the slope. Halfway to the ridge, MacDonald and Sam took Samantha from him. She was stirring fitfully by this time, and when she reached the crest, Kersten was waiting to help her back to her wagon. Fully conscious by this time, Samantha was no longer screaming. In fact, she seemed quite calm, even serene.

Back atop the ridge, Canyon picked up his Henry. But apparently he no longer needed it. The Blackfoot were pulling out.

"How do you like them apples?" Sam said, hurrying over to him. "The bastards are giving up. And it was Samantha did it."

Canyon nodded wearily. With their war chief struck down, the rest of the Blackfoot were streaming across the grassland to their ponies, carrying their dead with them. And Sam was right. It was Samantha's crazed charge that had done it—that and a well-aimed shot from a Kentucky rifle.

"Where's Gettis?" Canyon said.

"Over there," Sam said.

Canyon turned his head. Gettis and the judge were standing with MacDonald, Bill Walsh, and a few others, all of them watching the Blackfoot leave. The smiles on their faces resembled those of condemned men who have just been pardoned.

Canyon left Sam and walked over to Gettis. "Like to talk to you for a minute," Canyon told him.

"Sure."

The two men walked apart, both of them watching the Indians disappear to the north. They had difficulty taking their eyes off the departing warriors, it was such a pleasant sight.

"That was your shot that stopped Red Feather, wasn't it?"

"He was ready to cut you down. He had a throwing knife in his hand."

"So I guess I owe you."

"Don't worry about it."

"I wouldn't—if it were only the first time."

"What do you mean by that?" Jake asked.

"You going to pretend you don't know?"

"That's right. I don't know."

"That Kentucky rifle of yours can reach out a far piece, and that's the truth of it. Not too long ago, a week or so back, it reached out the way it did today, and when I looked up, the Blackfoot who had me by the throat was missing half his head. You going to pretend you didn't kill him?"

Gettis shrugged. "You're right. I fired the shot."

"You followed me from the wagon train, armed."

"I did."

"Why?"

"My ass was sore from sitting so long on a wagon seat."

"So you took your Kentucky rifle and followed me."

148

"Maybe I wanted to help you bring down some game," Gettis said.

"Maybe."

"If you don't believe me, you don't have to."

"I think maybe I'll believe you—for now."

"That's real decent of you."

"Twice now you've saved my Irish ass."

"I told you before. Don't worry about it."

"Well, I do a bit. You see, it makes things a mite difficult for me."

"That so?"

"You and Langley've come a long ways in a big hurry."

"Yes, we have. And you've come after us in just as big a hurry."

Canyon should have been surprised at Gettis' words, but he wasn't. The man was sharp enough to have figured things out.

"How long did you know that, Gettis?"

"Since you rode alongside our wagon and asked all them fool questions."

Canyon chuckled. "I thought I was being real careful."

"You were. Too careful. Besides, I know our Mr. Philbrick. And how anxious he is to stop the judge. I been waiting to see who he'd send. How much is he paying you?"

"Expenses."

Gettis frowned. "I don't believe you. But whatever he's paying, we will double the amount."

"I'm not for hire."

Gettis laughed shortly, bitterly. "You can say that—and work for a man like Philbrick?"

"I work for the president."

"The president? You must be out of your mind. Why would the president send you after the judge?"

"For trying to assassinate him. Myself, I think it's a damn good reason."

Astonished at Canyon's reply, Gettis studied Canyon carefully, as if he were waiting for Canyon to indicate he was not serious. It was clear Gettis found it impossible to take at face value Canyon's statement that the president was behind his mission—or that an attempt on the president's life was the reason for it.

"You telling me someone tried to assassinate the president?" Gettis asked Canyon carefully. "Are you serious, man?"

"I am. It was not successful, obviously."

"And this attempt to assassinate the president was supposed to have been engineered by the judge?"

"Yes."

"You must be mad to believe such a thing."

"I was given a file. It contained the statements of two of the other conspirators, along with much additional evidence. All of it incriminating the judge."

Gettis smiled coldly. "And this lovely material was provided by the honorable Denton Philbrick, I suppose."

"Yes."

"With Captain Jeremy Bullock also in attendance, I'll wager. I'd like to see that file."

"I'm sorry. I destroyed it."

"No you didn't," Gettis said shrewdly. "You're too smart a man to do anything as foolish as that. You figured you just might need that file to cover your ass."

Canyon made no effort to deny what Gettis said.

"I'm telling you you're making a mistake," Gettis went on. "Denton Philbrick is using you for his own purposes. This has nothing to do with an attempt on the president's life. Hell, I doubt such a thing ever occurred."

"I find that hard to believe."

"Of course you do. But you owe me, O'Grady. And that means you owe the judge as well."

Sam Wilder hurried up, leading two horses, his own and Canyon's.

"What're you two palaverin' about?" the small mountain man demanded, a grin on his face. "Let's go, hoss. The wagons're pulling out. MacDonald's itinerary shows once we get through that pass, in two weeks the next stop'll be Pendleton in the Umatilla Valley—and after that, Portland. Let's roll!"

As Canyon mounted the appaloosa, he looked down at Gettis. "You're right, Gettis," he said, "I owe you. I'll stay clear of you until we reach Portland. We'll continue this discussion then. Just don't try to pull anything before we get there."

Gettis stepped back without comment, his hard eyes locked onto Canyon as he watched him ride off with Sam Wilder.

9

Portland was a disappointment to Canyon, a gray, soggy town with rutted, muddy lanes passing for streets. Fronting them were newly constructed framed houses and buildings, most of which needed paint badly. Not long after he arrived, he left his hotel and went looking for a saloon called the Illahee, a name he took no pleasure at all in pronouncing. He found it down a narrow side street and pushed into it.

He found himself in a long, oblong room, its flooring fashioned of weather-beaten boards, covered with filthy sawdust, stained liberally with tobacco juice. On one side of the room was a dance floor, on the other a long bar, against which the saloon's patrons were crowded shoulder to shoulder. At the edge of the dance floor a narrow hallway led to the cribs of the house girls. The Indian girls providing the entertainment looked reasonably well scrubbed, their hair combed out and cut evenly across their backs. Aside from that, however, there was little else to recommend them—except that here in Portland, as Canyon overheard one sailor in the hotel lobby complain, there was barely one female for every ten males.

Canyon found a table along the back wall and slumped into it. An Indian bar girl hurried over and, after giggling and winking at him grotesquely, took his order for a beer. When it came, he found it almost too warm for his taste.

The dance floor was crowded with couples stomping and jumping clumsily to the sprightly tinkle of the saloon's piano. Every once in a while a small gent with a trumpet would join in with the piano player. The loggers and sailors and their short, chunky Indian partners paid little attention to the music, however, intent only on pawing one another until it came time to head for the cribs.

Canyon's instructions were for him to wait in this saloon until the two secret service men showed up. Since they had no idea when Canyon would arrive in Portland, Canyon was to show up at the same time every day for an hour or so until a connection was made. Canyon had arrived in town late the night before and this was his first visit to the saloon. He was hoping he would not have to repeat the chore for more than a few days, and was gratified when he saw two men, in suits that had a definite eastern cut to them, enter the saloon, look quickly around, and then start for his table.

They paused in front of Canyon's table and stared down at him expectantly, waiting for Canyon's prescribed greeting. The one closest to the table was a short, chunky, powerfully built fellow who sported a chocolate-brown derby hat, dark tie, high stiff collar, and white cuffs that gleamed from under the sleeves of his smartly tailored gray suit. His taller companion wore a derby hat also, white shirt and tie, and was dressed in a dark, neatly pressed suit.

His dark eyes were cold and calculating, his thin mouth a cruel emotionless line.

Canyon let them stand there for a moment before beginning the formalities.

"Been here long, gents?"

"Yeah," said the short one.

"And how do you like the weather?"

"It's too wet."

The two men relaxed and Canyon leaned back in his chair and waved at the two empty chairs at his table.

"Sit down, gents," he said. "Take a load off your feet."

The two men took off their derby hats and sat down.

"So you're Canyon O'Grady?" the taller one asked.

"Don't I look like him?"

"How the hell are we supposed to know what you look like?"

"That's right, you wouldn't." Canyon smiled. "Since you have the advantage on me, do you mind introducing yourselves?"

"I'm Jim Dillon," the tall one told him. "This little runt beside me is Mike Whitmore."

Whitmore allowed himself a thin smile at his partner's rude description of him. Neither one offered to shake Canyon's hand.

"Let's get this over with," said Whitmore. "I'm eager to get out of this fleabag of a town."

"How long you been here?"

"Close to three weeks. The worst of it was that trip across Panama. It was no picnic, I can tell you."

"It was no picnic on the trail to Oregon, either."

"Didn't say it was. So let's get on with it. You got the bastard?"

"You mean Langley?"

"We mean Judge Fowler G. Langley," said Jim Dillon, leaning closer to Canyon, a mean smile creasing his thin face. "Now, do you have the son of a bitch, or don't you?"

"I have him, but what's the hurry? Relax."

Dillon glanced around him. "I don't like this place and I don't like Portland. Didn't you hear my friend here? We want to get this over with. We've waited in this sinkhole long enough."

"Not to mention that trip across Panama," Canyon reminded him, sipping his warm beer.

Whitmore looked shrewdly at Canyon. "What's the matter, O'Grady?"

"What do you mean?"

"You're stalling us. You sure you have Langley?"

"Well, he's not sitting in my back pocket, if that's what you mean."

"That ain't what I meant. Quit stalling," Whitmore said.

"Where is he?" asked Dillon, his dark eyes cold, probing.

"He's not in Portland."

"I didn't ask where he wasn't."

"I got him in a safe place down river."

"What about his sidekick?"

"Jake Gettis?"

"Yeah, Gettis. He with the judge?"

"He's with him."

Dillon looked at his partner. "I don't like that."

"I don't care what you like, Jim," Whitmore said pleasantly, a cold smile on his face. "That ain't important.'' He looked back at Canyon. ''Who's got him in custody?''

''A friend of mine. Sam Wilder.''

''He up to holdin' the judge, is he?''

''He's the toughest man I know. He could tame a grizzly with a willow switch if he had to.''

''All right, then. Let's go get the judge.''

''There's just one thing,'' said Canyon.

''What's that?'' Whitmore asked impatiently.

''How do I know you two guys are who you say you are? You've shown me no identification and you ain't asked for mine. Let's see your papers.''

Dillon looked at his partner. ''I think he really is stalling.''

''Never mind that,'' said Whitmore, reaching into his breast pocket. ''Show him what he wants.''

Canyon examined both men's papers and saw that they were genuine, the IDs matching for each man. They were indeed on official government business; at least that was what their warrants said, and the signature on the bottom of each document was that of Denton Philbrick, assistant to the president. It was the same signature that was on Canyon's orders.

''Don't you want to see my papers?'' Canyon asked.

Whitmore was getting impatient. ''If you were in here waiting for us and knew the goddamn password—and know enough now to ask us for our papers—that makes you genuine enough for us. Now let's get on with it, O'Grady. No more stalling. Take us to Langley.''

''I've got a question first.''

Whitmore glared at him. ''What is it now?''

"Just where's this military trial supposed to take place?"

"Fort Hancock."

"Where's that?"

"In California, just outside San Francisco."

"How're you taking him there?"

"By schooner. You didn't think we were going to walk, did you?"

"I thought you might take the stage."

"Hell, that'd be worse than walking."

Canyon got to his feet. "All right, gents. Let's go. But I warn you, there's no boat to where we're going. You'll have to ride."

"How far is it?"

"Twenty miles."

"We'll rent a buggy," said Dillon. "Ain't no way you're goin' to get us on a horse."

Canyon shrugged and followed the two secret service agents out of the saloon.

Canyon did his best to keep pace with the surrey Dillon and Whitmore had hired, but it was slow going, the wheel ruts on the primitive, muddy roads making it exceedingly difficult to get up any speed. Not only that, but the surrey's wheels sent a constant shower of mud clots into the air, and Canyon found it wise to spur ahead, then wait for the surrey to catch up, after which he would again ride ahead. The two men paid little attention, therefore, when at the end of their journey they found Canyon waiting for them astride his horse in front of the gate leading to an old farmhouse.

As the two secret service men followed in behind Canyon, they passed the wagon that had taken the judge and Jake Gettis over the mountains. In light of the tremendous distance it had covered along with the weight of its cargo, they found its relatively small size hard to believe. Its side panels were cracked or broken, its canvas torn, and its wheels had lost some of their spokes. Sitting there, sagging dispiritedly into the hub-deep mud, it resembled an ancient campaigner ready now for the old soldiers' home.

Dillon reined up in front of the barn and the two men climbed down out of the surrey. Putting down the leather valise he carried, Whitmore stretched gratefully, his bones creaking after the long, uncomfortable ride.

Canyon had already led his mount into the barn and strode out of it now as the two men peered at the large farmhouse. It was dusk by this time and lamps in the first floor sent a soft yellow glow over the front yard.

"This way, gents," Canyon told them. "I'll send someone out to see to your horses."

"I hope there's coffee inside," said Whitmore.

"And something to eat," added Dillon. "It's too late now to make it back to Portland before nightfall."

"Stay the night," Canyon told them. "There's plenty of room."

"Maybe we'll do that," said Whitmore.

No one greeted them as Canyon pushed into the house. He marched ahead of them down a long, dusty hall and turned into a small back room. Inside it, sitting on separate cots were Judge Langley and Jake Gettis. In a corner, watching his two prisoners gloomily from a wooden chair tipped back against the wall, a long Kentucky rifle in his hand, sat Tim

Flannery. The old mountain man still looked like hell, his face a mess, but he was on the mend and was fit enough for his present task.

As Canyon and the two men entered the room, Sam Wilder appeared behind them and followed them in, crowding the room somewhat.

"Well, well, well, Judge," Whitmore said. "You came a long way to get nowhere."

"Hello, Whitmore."

"You know him?" Canyon asked the judge.

"Jake and I know them both," the judge told him. "They're hirelings. They aren't secret service agents at all. They get their paychecks from Denton Philbrick."

"I saw their papers," Canyon told him. "They looked genuine enough."

"Forgeries always do, O'Grady," Judge Langley said.

Dillon looked carefully around at Canyon. "These two men here all you got holding the judge?"

"That's right," Canyon told him.

"Just you and these two?" Whitmore repeated.

"You heard me."

"You think they're enough?"

"They're more than enough."

"I have handcuffs," Whitmore said. "I suggest we use them now."

Canyon shrugged. "If you think it's necessary."

"I do," said Whitmore.

Whitmore opened his valise and pulled forth two pairs of handcuffs. He strode over to the judge and told him to put his hands behind his back, then slipped the cuffs over his wrists. Glaring at Whitmore, Gettis allowed the man to handcuff him as well. With both men cuffed, Whitmore seemed re-lieved.

"Now," he said, turning to Canyon, "where's that coffee?"

Canyon glanced at Sam. "What about it, Sam?"

"You're right on time. I've got some fresh brewed in the kitchen."

"Lead the way."

Before following the others out the door, Canyon glanced over at Flannery, who was still sitting with his back to the wall. "You going to be all right, Tim?"

"With these two handcuffed, I won't have no trou-ble."

"We'll bring you some coffee."

"I'd appreciate that."

In the kitchen Canyon and the two agents slumped into chairs around the table while Sam poured the steaming coffee into their mugs and planted them in front of them. There was no milk or cream, but a jar of honey sat on the table. Dillon and Whitmore helped themselves from the honey jar and said not a word as they downed their coffee.

When they finished, Dillon glanced at Sam. "You the cook, too?"

"When I have to be."

"My partner here is famished," Whitmore said. "See what you can rustle up for him."

"I got some beans and bacon. Won't take long for me to fry 'em."

"Do it."

"Sure thing," Sam said, getting to his feet.

Whitmore looked at Canyon. "You said you'd send someone out to tend to our horses."

"Sam can't do everything."

"Maybe we'd better go out and see to them," Whitmore suggested to Canyon. "I don't want them to give out on us on our way back to Portland."

"Sure."

As Sam got busy at the stove, Canyon led the two men out of the farmhouse. It was completely dark by now and the horses were stamping impatiently in their traces as the men approached.

"I'll go fork some fresh straw into their stalls," Canyon told them.

"All right," said Whitmore. "You do that. I'll bring in the horses." Not long after, Whitmore led the two horses into the barn, then paused, peering into the gloom to find Canyon. The only light was a single kerosene lamp hanging from a post beside the door.

"Over here," Canyon called, putting aside his pitchfork.

Whitmore started up again, the horses clopping loudly on the plank floor as they followed after him. Buckets of water Canyon had filled stood to one side of the two stalls. He stepped aside as Whitmore backed in the horses; then he placed the buckets down in front of each stall. He was straightening up, about to ask if Whitmore was going to leave the surrey outside, when Dillon came softly up behind him and struck him on the back of his head with the barrel of his revolver.

The last thing Canyon remembered was a horse's forelegs stepping nervously back out of his way as he sprawled facedown onto the stall's freshly spread straw.

* * *

The back of his head pounding viciously, Canyon awoke to find himself outside the barn, sprawled on the ground, caught in the glare of an enormous and brilliant moon that seemed to be hovering only inches above his head. And just in front of him Tim Flannery and Sam Wilder were digging graves. Five of them.

Squinting up at the moon's near-blinding glare, Canyon's senses cleared enough for him to realize that the moon was a lantern held by Jim Dillon, whose revolver was trained on Flannery and Sam. Beside Dillon stood Whitmore, Canyon's Henry cradled in his arms. Langley and Gettis were propped against two pines, watching grimly as the two mountain men dug their graves.

Canyon stirred, considering the advisability of reaching up and grabbing Dillon. But his movement was detected.

Dillon turned quickly and placed the muzzle of his revolver inches from Canyon's face. "Go ahead, O'Grady," Dillon taunted. "Make your move."

"What's the matter with you?" Canyon demanded. "I can see you finishing off the judge and Gettis. But why me? Hell, I'm on your side. I led you to them, didn't I?"

"Don't take it personal, O'Grady. Just following orders. Philbrick and the captain want you out of it, too. Wouldn't do for you to show up in Washington and start asking questions."

"Damn you," Canyon snarled.

Evidently feeling good at how well things were

going, Dillon took a short step back, then kicked Canyon viciously in the side. Canyon twisted and swallowed the pain, making no effort to fight back. Instead, keeping his head down, he worked his way across the grass to the judge and Gettis.

"That's it," Dillon said, watching him go. "Go find a place to hide. I promise. You won't have long to wait."

Canyon glared back at him, then looked over at Sam and Tim. He could see they were dogging it, but even so they had just about finished digging the graves.

"You heard that?" Canyon asked the judge. "What he said about Philbrick and Captain Bullock."

"We heard," the judge whispered bitterly.

"Makes everything pretty clear. I'd hate like hell for them two to get away with this."

"I wouldn't like it much, either," said Gettis.

"We thought you were out for good," the judge told Canyon.

"From the way my head feels, I should have been," Canyon muttered. "I didn't expect them to make their move that quick. What about you two?"

"As soon as you left the house with them," Gettis told him, "Sam took the keys in Whitmore's valise and unlocked our cuffs. We've still got the cuffs on, but they're not locked. We've been waiting for the right time to make our move."

"The thing is," whispered Langley, "they have the guns. Walked right in and disarmed Tim before he could do a thing."

Canyon understood their dilemma perfectly. All they had for weapons now were their bare hands and Sam and Tim's two shovels. They had stripped Canyon of his revolver when they knocked him out, and Whitmore had the Henry. That was a lot of firepower to go against bare hands and shovels.

"We'll have to hit them all at once."

"Now, how in hell do we manage that?" Gettis asked.

"I just had an idea. Whatever I say, listen and pay attention."

"What the hell are you up to?"

"Watch—and listen."

Canyon cleared his throat loudly. There was no response from Dillon or Whitmore. Canyon cleared his throat a second time, more loudly. Whitmore glanced in his direction.

"You sure you know how to use that rifle, Whitmore?"

"I know how."

"You know, I've been wondering. What would happen if we all came at you two at the same time?"

Dillon swung around to face Canyon. "Shut your mouth, O'Grady."

"What I mean," Canyon continued, ignoring Dillon, "is there's only the two of you standing there. But there's five of us. Now, if I were to count to three, say, and we rushed you, you'd have a devil of a time figuring which one of us to shoot first."

"I wouldn't have no trouble at all, Irishman," Dillon said. "I'd figure it out."

"Oh, I'm sure you would."

"Besides," said Whitmore. "There's two of you handcuffed. You're only bluffing, O'Grady."

"Maybe. But them shovels have sharp blades and that Henry you got in your hand isn't all that quick in close quarters."

"Keep it up," Dillon said evenly. "And I'll finish you off right now."

Canyon shrugged. "Isn't that what you got planned anyway? The way I see it, we might as well have at you now instead of waiting like sheep to get dumped into them graves."

Whitmore looked nervously at Dillon and then raised the Henry.

"I mean," Canyon went on, getting slowly to his feet, "we might as well make this here burial party interesting."

Dillon took a step back. "I said shut up!"

"Maybe on the count of three would do it."

Dillon thumb-cocked his revolver and Whitmore edged closer to Dillon. They evidently considered Canyon more of a threat than their two obedient grave-diggers.

"One," said Canyon.

"Damn you," cried Dillon, lifting his revolver.

"Two . . ."

"Hey!" Sam cried, raising his shovel over his shoulder. "Lower that revolver, Dillon."

Startled, Dillon glanced at Sam.

"Three," cried Canyon, launching himself at Whitmore.

At the same instant Sam and Tim swung the blades of their shovels down onto Dillon's extended arm.

His revolver went off, the slug plowing into one of the empty graves.

Canyon grabbed the Henry's barrel and shoved it skyward, the rifle detonating harmlessly into the air. Behind him, Judge Langley and Gettis swarmed over Whitmore. After snatching the rifle from his grasp, Gettis swung the stock around with vicious force. He caught Whitmore on the side of his head, slamming him backward into one of the graves. By this time a constant howl of pain was coming from Dillon as he held on to his shattered arm and sank to his knees.

It was over that quickly.

Three weeks later Canyon escorted Jim Dillon and Mike Whitmore to the clipper ship that would return them to the East Coast. The ship's captain had been deputized and was responsible for delivering the two men to waiting secret service agents in the port of Baltimore. Gettis and Judge Langley had had a choice in the matter and had selected the clipper ship, whose route would take it around the Cape—a formidable, grueling passage that should make the trip across Panama seem like a stroll in a park by comparison. As the majestic sailing ship left on the tide, Canyon, Jake Gettis, and the judge retired to a dockside grog shop.

"Canyon, there's one question I've been meaning to ask you," Judge Langley said after their drinks arrived.

"Now's your chance," said Canyon.

"How did you come to believe that Jake and I were not assassins?"

Canyon glanced at Gettis and smiled. "Jake had a pretty good idea who I was when he saw that Blackfoot throttling me. But he saved my life with that long Kentucky rifle of his and later, when I was hauling Samantha back to the ridge, he saved my ass again."

"That's Jake. What about me?"

"A man should be known by his associates. And his friends. Jake is no assassin, and it follows you aren't either. I didn't have to think very hard on that one."

"Only you let us wonder until we got here."

"Just being cautious."

"I swear, Canyon," Gettis said, "you cut a pretty fine line out there at the farmhouse. You near got us all killed."

Canyon shrugged. "We had to make those men show their true colors. And I didn't know any other way to find out what Philbrick really had in mind for you two."

"That file they gave you is going back with the clipper ship's captain," the judge added. "It was a good thing you saved it instead of destroying it. Does that mean you were suspicious of Philbrick and the captain from the beginning?"

"I am always a little suspicious."

The judge laughed, obviously approving such an attitude. "You'll be interested to know that both men are now in custody, blabbing their fool heads off. It seems they were not the only members of the president's administration involved in this matter. Conspiracy to murder is the charge, but of course the proceedings against them will be kept quiet."

"Too bad. The way I see it, such men should be hung publicly."

"Perhaps, but this is how the president has been advised to proceed. One more thing, Canyon," the judge went on, "I think you should know that I received a rather lengthy communication from the president. It arrived yesterday on the afternoon packet from San Francisco. The president wants me to personally thank you for your efforts on our behalf."

"And on his behalf too, as I understand it."

"Yes, of course," the judge admitted, smiling. "As a member of the president's party out here, I have been informed that next spring they will be sending me back to Washington as one of Oregon's senators—and I'll be one of the president's strongest congressional allies. He will then have the votes necessary to prevent any attempt by his opponents to impeach him."

"Impeachment, is it?" said Canyon, shaking his head. "Sure, and I'll never be able to figure out politics."

"Don't try, Canyon," said the judge. "Don't even try. It's no chore for an honest man."

"Where does that leave you, Judge?"

"We won't go into that."

Gettis spoke up then. "Canyon, I hear you're going back East overland. Why don't you go by way of Panama? It'll be a lot quicker and a lot safer."

"Maybe so, but I left my palomino in the livery at Fort Billings. You might say I'm going back to ransom him."

"With what?"

"With that appaloosa Chief Stalking Bear gave me."

"When will you be leaving?"

"I've got to say good-bye to Kersten first. I'll be visiting with her tomorrow at her brother's place down the coast."

"I don't envy you that task," said the judge. "It is my feeling that she puts great store by you."

"It's a fact, Judge. She wants me to stay out here. But this country is too wet for me."

Shortly thereafter, the three finished their drinks and left the saloon. Out on the sidewalk Canyon shook both men's hands, wished them good luck, and bid them good-bye. As he walked off, a light drizzle began to fall, making him absolutely certain that his decision to put Portland behind him was a sound one.

Twirling her parasol, Kersten kept just ahead of Canyon as they left the cliff overlooking the Pacific and mounted the broad veranda of her brother's new home. Situated on a wooded knoll high above the Pacific, it was an ideal site for a man who had spent most of his life at sea.

On the veranda there were two wicker chairs, a glass-topped table between them. Sinking into one of them, Canyon could smell the new, as-yet-unpainted wood of the veranda's flooring, and behind him the odor of fresh paint as two landlocked sailors on the other side of the house finished painting the big house's clapboard siding. They were painting it white. The trim and shutters, Kersten told him, would be a dark, forest green, making the house an exact replica of their family's home back in Maine.

An Indian woman brought out a tray with a pitcher of lemonade and two glasses, ice chips in a dish beside the pitcher. Placing it down on the glass table, she vanished back through the French doors.

"I have to admit," Canyon said, pouring himself a glass of lemonade and dropping a spike of ice into it. "That's a real spectacular view. But are you sure the beat of that surf won't keep you awake?"

She laughed. "Me, perhaps, but not my brother."

"Sort of a lullaby for him, huh?"

She nodded, then looked at him with somber eyes. "Canyon, have you really made up your mind? You're leaving this lovely country, going back East? Is there nothing I can say or do to dissuade you?"

He shook his head. "My mind's made up, Kersten."

"There's nothing I can say? Nothing I can do?"

"Afraid not. I'm heading back first thing tomorrow, before winter settles in. It comes fast in the mountains."

"I'll be thinking of you," she said.

"And I'll be thinking of you, too. I sure hope you'll be happy here, Kersten."

"Don't you fret, Canyon O'Grady. This is just the place for me. From what I gather, there are far more eligible males than females out here. As a result, we ladies are held in rather high esteem. I'll take my time, select a young man whose fortune is still ahead of him, and provide him with a fine home. I am sure I will make him a good and faithful wife. And I think I will like that."

"It does sound pretty good at that."

"The East is another, older world, and I no longer want to be part of it. I want this new world—this new ocean. I think I am going to be very happy here, Canyon."

"Maybe someday I'll come back and visit."

"If you do, you will be most welcome. Always. I wouldn't be sitting on this porch, sipping lemonade, if it weren't for you—and that terrible trip we took through the wilderness together."

"We had some fierce times. Yes, we did."

She finished her lemonade and stood up, and Canyon realized his visit was over. He was not certain, but he thought he caught the gleam of a tear on her cheek. But she lowered her parasol, so he couldn't be sure. Taking his arm, she led him off the veranda and around the house to the livery barn, where the old sailor who had brought him out here was waiting to take him back to his digs in Portland.

He kissed Kersten lightly on her cheek, felt the salt of her tears, swallowed hard, but said nothing as he climbed into the buggy and nodded to the driver. As the carriage's wheels crunched over the gravel, he turned and waved good-bye to Kersten. She returned his wave, then swung about and ran into the house.

Canyon settled back on the ribbed-leather seat, and not much later, the rutted road ahead of him obscured by a chill fog rolling in off the Pacific, he felt better about his decision to leave this country. He found himself thinking of Fern Song and the lodges of Stalking Bear's band. He was sure that on their way back to Fort Billings with him,

Wilder and Flannery would not be at all unhappy at the prospect of spending awhile in that Nez Percé valley.

And neither would Canyon.